ENCHANTRESS

COVEN: BOOK 6

DAVID NETH

 Publishing

Enchantress

Coven, Book 6

Copyright © 2021 by David Neth

Batavia, NY

www.DavidNethBooks.com

ISBN: 978-1-945336-19-5
First Edition

Subscribe to the author's newsletter for updates and exclusive content:
DavidNethBooks.com/Newsletter

Follow the author at:
www.facebook.com/DavidNethBooks

ALSO BY DAVID NETH

COVEN
HARPY
SIREN
VALKYRIE
SHAPESHIFTER
SORCERER
WITCH (SHORT STORY)
ENCHANTRESS
ORACLE
TRICKSTER

UNDER THE MOON
THE FULL MOON
THE HARVEST MOON
THE BLOOD MOON
THE CRESCENT MOON
THE BLUE MOON

THE ART OF MAGIC

FUSE
ORIGIN
OMERTÁ
OBLIVION

HEAT
BLACK MAGNET
DUST STORM
THE GATEKEEPER

STANDALONE
ALL I EVER WANTED

CHAPTER 1

- APRIL 1988 -

Scarlett walked through the commotion backstage of Shea's Performing Arts Center where stagehands, technicians, and managers all mingled in an effort to bring in the set pieces of *Me and My Girl* that had just arrived in Buffalo from their stop in Pittsburgh. It was organized chaos as different members of the crew pitched in to help make a new place out of the blank canvas that was the stage.

And what a stage it was! Scarlett's favorite thing whenever they arrived in a new city was walking on stage prior to showtime to get a sense of the place before she stepped out to perform. She loved standing beneath the tall, immaculate ceilings, being the center of attention, even if it was for an audience of none.

"Hey, get out of the way!" one of the stagehands called to Scarlett as they rolled in a large backdrop.

Scarlett took several steps backward and let out a yelp as she reached the edge of the stage.

Before panic could really set in, she felt a strong grip on her arm pull her back to her feet.

"Careful," a young man said with a smile. He wore a navy blue T-shirt and black work pants. Clipped to the top of his side pocket was a silver pocket knife. "You'll learn where the edge is after a few more trips." He released his grip and offered his hand. "I'm Oliver."

"Scarlett." The size of his arms suggested his strength, but she was surprised that his handshake was gentle.

"I know this sound forward, but I just have to say that you are gorgeous."

She could feel the heat rise to her face, especially as their hands remained locked together. "Well, if we're being strictly objective, I would have to say that you're not so bad yourself."

His cheeks turned up into a wider smile. "So why don't we take this from a formal observation to something a little more casual?"

Scarlett pulled her hand away. "Easy there, Oliver. I make it a general rule not to date locals. I'm always traveling on one show or another, which I very much enjoy. I'm never around long enough to make anything last—not to say that I don't have fun." She smirked at him.

He opened his arms. "Hey, maybe I'd be the one to make you stay."

She crossed her arms and looked him up and down, the smirk still present on her face. "You're going to have to try real hard to impress me."

"I never turn down a challenge."

Rolling her eyes, she turned away from him. "I'm going to go back to my hotel and rest up before rehearsals start tomorrow. It was nice meeting you."

"Take it easy, Scarlett," he said. "We'll be seeing more of each other!"

"Until my show rolls out of here at the end of next week."

Around the corner, Scarlett stepped into the rehearsal space and nearly collided with Ella, who played Lady Jackie in the show.

"Scarlett," she said very succinctly, as if her name were a command.

"Sorry, I wasn't paying attention."

"I can see that." Ella nodded back toward the stage where Oliver was moving sacks of sand, the muscles in his arms straining from the effort. "He's cute."

"That he is," Scarlett agreed. "And quite the charmer too."

"Oh, so you were talking to him?"

Scarlett nodded.

"Normally, I'd take that as you having dibs, but I know you have that silly rule about the locals, right?"

ENCHANTRESS

Another nod. "Yeah, and that's exactly what I told him."

Ella smoothed out the corners of her bright red lips, then fussed with her blonde hair. "Well, I have no such rule."

Scarlett motioned back toward the stage. "Then by all means, be my guest. But quite frankly, I don't think he'll go for you. He seems to have his eyes locked on me."

Both women looked over as Oliver noticed them watching. He waved and they each returned the gesture before he went back to work.

Ella pursed her lips. "We'll have to see who he chooses."

CHAPTER 2

- FEBRUARY 1989 -

Kathy zipped up her backpack and hauled it onto her shoulder. She already dreaded the long walk to the bus stop and the ride back to the stop near her house. Her back was nearly aching simply from the idea of lugging all of her books that far.

While she filed out of the classroom with the other students, she focused most of her energy on the discussion from class on American Literature during the Civil War, specifically Harriet Beecher Stowe. The crowd in the hallway didn't even register on her mind until she heard a familiar voice call her name.

"Kathy!"

Whipping her head around, she found herself face-to-face with Jeremy.

"Oh! I didn't even see you!"

He chuckled. "I called your name a few times."

"How did you know I would be here?"

"You told me you had class today, and Porreco College isn't that big," he said with a shrug. "Didn't take me long to find which one was yours."

"So you stalked me." She adjusted the strap on her shoulder.

"When you put it like that it sounds creepy. Here, let me take that."

Before she could protest, he pulled her bag off of her shoulders and lifted it onto his, which was an odd look for someone in a button-down shirt with a tie.

"Thanks." She looked him up and down. "You look nice. Did you just come from work?"

He nodded. "I thought maybe the two of us could go to dinner. I made reservations for five-thirty."

Kathy checked her watch. It was just after five and her stomach growled.

"Sounds like you're hungry."

She smiled. "I mean, I've gotta eat sometime."

"Then let's go." He started leading her down the hall toward the exit. "I found this great place in the city. Total neighborhood restaurant, great Italian food. You'll love it."

Kathy followed him out to his car and climbed in the passenger seat, just as if they'd never taken that six-month break. It was natural, spending time with Jeremy again. It was nice and familiar. She missed him.

They had reconnected at Samantha and Steven's wedding, which brought back a rush of emotions that got the better of them. That night they had hooked up for the first time since the breakup, but Kathy was adamant about taking things slow from then on. If they were going to get back together, she wanted to know that things would be different. Dinner was a good start.

The closest parking spot to the restaurant that Jeremy could find was half a block down Plum Street. If it weren't for the bitter temperatures and the chilling wind, Kathy wouldn't have minded the walk. As it was, they didn't say much on their brisk walk until they were inside the warm building.

"Hi, I have a reservation for two at five-thirty," Jeremy said to the hostess.

"Right this way." She led them to the back of the restaurant in a cozy corner.

The walls were adorned with old pictures of the family who owned the restaurant. Shots from throughout the years as the restaurant slowly evolved over time, polaroids from family vacations to Europe or to National Parks out west.

Kathy smiled at the sentiment. It was one of the things she loved about her own house. The history of it was hers and her family's. Nobody could take that away from them. It was nice to see the same pride of place here.

Jeremy and Kathy both scanned the menu in silence. The awkward tension between them built as more time passed. The waitress came over and they each ordered, Jeremy insisting on a beer. Kathy contemplated a beverage herself, but figured it was best to keep a level head during this conversation. Besides, when she got home she'd have to work on homework.

"So how's school?" Jeremy asked after the waitress left their table.

"Um…not bad." Kathy rubbed the back of her neck, then ran her fingers through her hair.

"But not great?"

"Well…"

"I'm surprised you're doing the whole college thing," he said. "I never thought you were interested."

She shrugged. "I mean, that's kind of always been the plan."

"Yeah, but that's always been Samantha's plan. Not necessarily yours."

"True, but what she says makes sense. I'll have a better shot of getting a better-paying job with a college degree."

"What do you think you want to do when you're done?"

The waitress came over and set a tall glass in front of him. He offered her a quick thanks and then reached for it to take a sip.

"I'm not sure yet," Kathy admitted. "I still haven't decided on a major."

"How long are they going to let you take classes without a major?"

"I don't know, but I took an English class last semester and

I liked it. I'm taking another one now and it's good. Maybe I can do something with that."

"With an English degree? What are you going to do, teach?"

She made a face. "I don't think I'm cut out to be a teacher."

Jeremy chuckled. "Then what are you going to do with that degree?"

"I don't know, Jeremy," she snapped. She turned her attention to the photos on the walls. One was a black and white photo of a group of kids standing beside a garden hose. Judging by their clothing, it looked to be a hot summer day.

He pushed his glass aside and leaned forward. "Sorry. Didn't mean to push any buttons. I just—I thought I would offer realistic scenarios."

"I know, but it's something that I'm constantly worried about. I want to start pulling my weight with the bills and everything so the sooner I figure out what I'm going to do, the better."

"That's fair," he said. "But you don't want to lose yourself in the process. Kathy, what I like most about you is that you don't care what other people think. You've always done your own thing."

She smiled. "Thanks. Anyway. So how's your new job? Where is it again? Blue Water Insurance?"

He nodded. "Yeah."

"How do you like it?"

"It pays well enough."

"But you don't *like* it…" She pinched her straw and leaned forward to take in a sip. "A bit like the pot calling the kettle black here, isn't it?"

That brought a grin to his face. "Touché. No, it's not terrible. It's similar to what I went to school for, but not quite. It's a stepping stone."

Kathy nodded. "Gotcha."

A stepping stone job was far from her reach. She was stuck jumping from one low-rung job to the next. But, like Jeremy said, until Samantha's nagging made her feel like that wasn't good enough, Kathy had been happy with all the other aspects of her life. And she always managed to get by when it came to money.

Jeremy studied the photos hanging on the wall while Kathy twirled her straw in her ice water. Apparently after covering their bases with their jobs, they had run out of things to talk about. That thought made her a bit sad.

Was there relationship that shallow before? She didn't think so, but then, they were always doing something the first time they dated. Going here or there, or seeing this person or that. There was rarely any time with just the two of them to sit down and talk. But whenever she needed someone to lean on, Jeremy had usually been there. It was that glimmer of hope that she clung to now.

"I suppose the awkward silence was inevitable," she joked.

He offered a polite smile. "There's a lot for us to catch up on.

Sounds like we've both changed a lot."

And yet the passion between us is still burning bright. Kathy thought back to the night of Samantha's wedding and her cheeks flushed a little.

After another few empty seconds passed, she decided to brave the question. "So what exactly are we doing?"

"You mean about us?"

"Yeah. We had that one-night stand, which I thought was great. But then we've been fumbling around each other ever since. It's been almost three weeks. When are we actually going to talk about it?"

Jeremy let out a heavy breath—clearly a ploy to buy time. He glanced toward the door and immediately stiffened up. Facing forward again, he kept his head low.

"What is it?"

She looked toward the door herself, but didn't see anyone at first. She scanned the room and her eyes landed on the woman sitting at the bar in a beautiful black dress. She was nursing a glass of wine and casually flipping through a magazine.

Kathy turned back to Jeremy, suddenly annoyed that an innocent woman minding her own business intruded into their dinner so completely.

"So do you want to tell me who that is?"

CHAPTER 3

Surprise!" Steven said with a big smile as he shifted the car in park.

Samantha looked out at all the monochromatic townhouses surrounding several small parking lots jutting off the winding road that seemed like a maze. It was just off one of the arterial roads out of the city, and directly across from Porreco College.

Nervously, she climbed out of the car. "What is this? I thought we were going to dinner?"

"We will. This is just a little detour."

From the nearest building, a man stepped out and zipped up his black puffy winter jacket. He grimaced in the cold, but plastered on a smile when he saw Steven, waving the hand that held a clipboard. "You must be the Harpers!"

Steven stepped forward and the two men greeted each other like old buddies.

"I'm Stuart Jemson, the property manager for Willowood Village." He turned to Samantha. "And you must be the new Mrs. Harper!"

Despite the ambush, being called by her new name brought a smile to Samantha's face and she shook Stuart's hand to be polite.

Stuart clapped his hands along his clipboard. "All right, we're taking a look at a three bedroom, two-and-a-half bath today. It's just across the way here, so we won't be in the cold too long."

He led them across to a nondescript building and let them in the door to the unit on the right.

There was plastic over the carpeting to give the impression that everything was newly-installed, but Samantha could see a few stains on the edges of the room, outlining where the previous tenets had had their furniture. Worse, the room had an odd smell, like fresh paint and cigarettes fused together.

Samantha felt her stomach go queasy and she brought her gloved hand to her nose for a moment to make sure she could hold down her lunch.

"This is one of our largest units," Stuart said. "There are three levels: the walk-out basement, the ground floor here, and a second story above. There are balconies on this level and the one below us. Upstairs, there's a master suite with a walk-in closet…"

Stuart continued talking as Samantha wandered throughout the apartment. It wasn't terrible, if she was being honest. It certainly needed to be aired out, but she knew several people who lived in apartments like these and loved it. The problem was, it wasn't her style.

Worse, Samantha thought that Steven had given up on the notion of the two of them getting their own place. To her, it didn't make sense to move out when she and Kathy already had a huge house—one that they owned free and clear.

This whole apartment tour came as a complete shock because Steven hadn't mentioned much about moving out since they really began planning their wedding. Guess it was something they hadn't ever discussed.

"The second bedroom upstairs is right next door to the master, making it a perfect place for the two of you to expand your family," Stuart went on.

Steven nodded. "Sounds great!"

"We also have several playgrounds on the property, so all the kids can play and the families get to know each other," he went on. "It's a real, true community."

But not my neighborhood, Samantha thought. She had always envisioned her kids would play in the same yard that she and Kathy had. That they'd draw sidewalk chalk on the steps where they passed out candy at Halloween or waited for the school bus. Samantha wanted the traditional idea of community, not the cardboard box version.

"And for both kids and adults, we have a community pool, which is perfect in the summertime," Stuart added.

Steven nudged Samantha's arm. "You always said you could use a pool when it's hot out. Now we have one!"

She gave a tight smile.

Apparently picking up on his wife's mood, Steven turned to Stuart and said, "Would you mind if we checked out the second floor on our own? I think we'd like to discuss some things between the two of us."

"Oh sure!" Stuart leaned against the counter in the kitchen. "You go right ahead and take all the time you need! I'll be right here when you're done!"

Steven smiled and led Samantha upstairs. They stepped into the nearest bedroom, a small one that overlooked the communal backyard, and Steven closed the door.

"So what do you think?"

Samantha raised her eyebrows, an argument about being blindsided on the tip of her tongue. "It's…it's kind of *bland.*"

Steven looked around at the pearly-white walls. "Looks like a clean slate, or a fresh start. Kind of like our marriage, right?" He wrapped his arms around her and they looked out the back window.

She squirmed in his grasp. "I'm not used to a clean slate. I'm used to living in my family's history—the place where I grew up."

"You just haven't lived anywhere else. Trust me, I thought it'd be weird when my parents sold the house that I grew up in—and it was for a little bit, but I adjusted. Things change, Sam. It doesn't mean it has to be bad."

"I know, but…" *But what about Kathy?* she thought. That point would not strengthen her argument for keeping their living arrangements the same. "I just can't picture myself living in this type of *community*."

"It's just a start," he said. "And think about the location. It's easy to get to everything—and right across from Kathy's school! She could stop by anytime."

Knowing that that offer would be short-lived, Samantha decided to side-step it instead.

"It's more than that, though. Where are the trees? Where's the neighborhood character?"

"It's with the people," Steven said. "We'll just have to get to know our new neighbors."

"In the community pool, where everyone's probably peed? I would seriously question that water."

"So avoid the pool."

"And like you said, Kathy's college is right across the street. It's still a new school and they don't have any dorms or anything. Soon this family-friendly neighborhood will be full of college kids partying at all hours of the night. If we start a family, I don't want our kids around that."

"So we'll move by time it gets that bad."

Samantha made a face and looked around the small room again. She could picture a crib and some toys in the corner, but in her head they were someone else's. Not hers. "I don't know, Steven."

He huffed. "Fine. I'll go tell Stuart to forget the whole thing. I just thought *I* would bring an option to the table for a change." Turning, he crossed the small hallway to the stairs and left her standing alone.

CHAPTER 4

- MARCH 1988 -

When Scarlett got back down to the lobby of her hotel, she was hating herself for letting her rivalry with Ella bend her own rule. Yesterday, after Scarlett had told Ella to take a shot with Oliver, he had promptly turned Ella's offer down.

If nothing else, Oliver made one thing clear: his sights were set on Scarlett. He had been persistent in his requests to take her out and, after seeing Ella's rejection, Scarlett accepted his offer simply to rub it in Ella's face later.

Now that the time had come for her to come through on her promise to go out with him, she debated whether she should. After all, she had created the "don't date locals" rule for a reason. If nothing else, she had decided she was *not* going to tell anyone in the cast or crew. The last thing she needed was to be ridiculed for a rule they all made fun of her for to begin with.

Oliver rose to his feet when she stepped off the elevator and he met her halfway across the room. "You look beautiful."

She smiled and thanked him, even though impressing him wasn't her plan. She had opted for black pants and a nice top under her puffy jacket in an effort to look nice. Even though it was March, it was still cold so practicality needed to beat out fashion.

Oliver offered his arm and led them out of the hotel. He wore a button-down shirt tucked in to his black jeans. She could see a silver chain peeking out from beneath his shirt, and clipped to the inside of his front jeans pocket was the silver pocket knife she had seen back at the venue. Over top, he wore a khaki jacket. His look told her that he made an effort but still wanted to be comfortable.

"I see you're always prepared," she said when they stepped out into the early-spring air. "What's with the pocket knife?"

He looked down at it then smiled at her. "Hey, you never know when you're going to need it."

"That's always a concern of mine," she said dryly.

"Don't worry, when you're with me I've got you covered."

Noting that he didn't seem to pick up on her sarcasm—or maybe he just decided not to comment on it—she asked, "Where are we going to eat?"

"There's a bar just up here," he said as they crossed Delaware

Avenue to stay on Chippewa. "They have local bands play live music every night, but that doesn't start for another hour. I wanted to make sure we had time to talk at dinner."

"This is just dinner," Scarlett clarified as they reached the bar. "It's not a date."

"It's not a date yet," he said as he held the door open for her.

They stepped inside and grabbed a table by the window overlooking the street. An easy getaway if Oliver decided not to back off. To hell with what Ella would say. Scarlett had decided she was not going to break her own rule.

After they ordered, they were both quiet until Oliver broke the silence.

"I bet you've tried a lot of different food from all over the place."

She shrugged. "Not really, actually. We eat at a lot of fast food places, delis, that kind of thing."

"Really?"

"Yeah, there's not usually a lot of time to eat out. And, like I said, I don't date locals."

"And yet you've made the exception for me."

She shook her head. "This is not a date. Just two people having a meal together."

"Sounds like a date to me."

"A date would be if we did something after dinner, or if we were trying to figure out if we have a connection, or if we held hands or kissed or something."

"Been a while since you've been on a date, hasn't it?"

Scarlett scoffed. "It hasn't been that long!"

"Well, if you never date locals and you haven't dated anyone on tour with you, I can't imagine how you would meet someone."

"This is getting—what about you? When was the last date you were on?"

He looked up at the ceiling as he thought about it. "Um…last month. I went on a date with a girl who just moved into my apartment building. We met in the laundry room."

"That's cute."

"Didn't work out."

"Obviously, because here we are."

Oliver smiled. "Oh, so you're admitting this is a date?"

She opened her mouth to reply, then closed it and looked toward the kitchen. "Where's our food? It's been a while."

"I'm just saying, there's no sense in you traveling all over the place if you don't get out and see the cities you visit."

"Yes, you've already convinced me of that," she said. "That's why I'm here. But to be honest, I could go to any dive bar in any city. What makes this one specific to Buffalo?"

"It's not just this bar, but it's part of the experience."

"I'm not buying what you're selling here."

"After dinner I'll take you around."

She cocked an eyebrow. "Show me a good time?"

"Only if you want to."

Their food arrived and the conversation lulled. By the end of the meal, the live music began, making conversation impossible. They listened to a few songs before Oliver reached for her hand and nodded toward the door. She pulled on her coat and followed him.

"It was getting kind of loud in there," he told her once they were outside and away from the noise.

"Yeah, I'm getting kind of tired anyway," she said.

"Tired already? You haven't even seen the city yet!"

She checked her watch and saw it was just after eight o'clock. It was early to turn in, even if she did have a long day of rehearsals in the morning. "As long as I'm back by ten, eleven tops."

He smiled. "Deal."

They took a cab up a few miles to Allentown, where Oliver took her into another bar. But this one wasn't as laid-back as the last one. Everyone was up on their feet dancing to the music that was blaring.

Oliver led them to a bar top table that they claimed as their own. He leaned in close to Scarlett's ear. "You want anything to drink?"

"Just one drink." She needed to lean in close for him to hear her. When she did, she smelled his aftershave, which she hadn't noticed before. It was nice.

He disappeared into the crowd and came back a few minutes later with a glass of wine and a beer for himself. "You look like a girl who enjoys one of these on occasion."

She grinned, feeling a flutter in her stomach because of how well he seemed to know her already.

Easy girl, she told herself. *Don't get too attached. I'll be out of town by next week.*

When they finished their drinks, Oliver leaned in close again and asked, "Do you want to dance?"

Without a word, she took his hand and led him into the crowd, where they moved to the music of Duran Duran, Blue Mercedes, and Bobby Brown.

They lost track of time and when Oliver pulled her aside, she realized how parched she was.

"It's 10:30," he said close to her ear.

"Guess we better get going," she said, disappointment slipping into her voice. She only hoped her tone was muted by the music.

Outside, they managed to grab a cab that took them back to Scarlett's hotel, where he walked her to the lobby.

"You want me to walk you up?" he asked.

She thought of Ella, or any of the other girls, and knew that if they saw her with Oliver that she wouldn't hear the end of her breaking her own rule.

"No, that's okay. Thanks for tonight, though. I had a really good time."

"See what happens when you give in a little?"

She rolled her eyes and smiled. "Don't ruin the moment, Oliver."

"I'll see you tomorrow at the theater."

"Sounds good."

He hesitated, then went for it, kissing her on the lips. Only a moment, but long enough to send the message that this was no cheek kiss. When he pulled away, he searched her face for permission to try again.

"I'll see you tomorrow," Scarlett said, then turned and stepped to the elevator.

CHAPTER 5

Jeremy stared at the woman at the bar, then back at Kathy, speechless.

"Obviously you know her," Kathy said. "Who is she?"

He turned to reach back for his coat. "Do you want to go somewhere else?"

Kathy leaned back in her chair and crossed her arms. "Jeremy, answer me: who is she?" Her voice grew loud enough to draw attention, including the mysterious woman at the bar.

Turning, the woman flashed a bright smile and waved at Jeremy, who timidly waved back. Before Kathy could realize what was going on, the woman stood beside their table with her glass of wine in her hand.

"I had no idea you were here!" She rubbed Jeremy's

shoulder and left it there possessively, raising it only to extend her hand toward Kathy. "I'm Lisa."

"Nice to meet you. I'm Kathy."

Lisa's hand returned right to Jeremy's shoulder. "Do you work with Jeremy?"

She shook her head. "No, I don't. Actually, we—"

"We're friends," he said quickly, then added, "So is Lisa."

Kathy tucked both her lips between her teeth and nodded. "Mmm."

"I'm just killing time waiting for one of my girlfriends to get out of work," Lisa said to Jeremy. "She lives around the corner on 31st and I just figured I'd stop for a quick glass of wine. It's been a long day. And to think, we still have two more days before the weekend." She turned to Kathy and gave an exaggerated groan. "I need a drink halfway through the week just to get me through the rest." She swatted Jeremy's arm and pointed to his beer. "You're the same way!"

Definitely Jeremy's type, Kathy thought to herself. Outwardly, she gave her own polite smile, avoiding eye contact with Jeremy. She wanted to make this as painful for him as it was for her.

"What time does she get out of work?" Jeremy asked.

Lisa finished a big sip. "Six o'clock, which means I should probably get going. Have to bundle up in this cold, you know? It's brutal this year!"

"Mmm," Kathy mumbled as Lisa downed the rest of her glass.

"Well, it was nice meeting you, Kathy," she said. "And Jeremy, don't have too many of those." Again, she pointed to his beer and laughed.

Jeremy and Kathy were quiet as they watched Lisa close out her tab, wrap her scarf around her neck, and button up her jacket.

"I'm sorry," Jeremy said after Lisa had stepped through the front door. "I had no idea she'd be here."

Kathy stared down at the empty table. Her angry performance stunted by the arrival of the waitress with their food, requiring Kathy to politely thank her before turning her attention back to Jeremy.

With her initial tactic having been ruined, she tried another. "So are you dating her?"

Jeremy quickly took a sip of his drink, which annoyed Kathy at first. But then, had she and Jeremy discussed if they were actually dating? Did she have any claim on him to be annoyed that he was seeing another girl? It had only been three weeks since they reconnected and they'd both kept each other at arm's length, even though the attraction could not be denied.

She sighed. "No, I can't be mad at you if you are. Our lives had been completely separate up until Samantha's wedding and now…" She shrugged, knowing he'd understand the meaning.

"Well, thank you for that," he said. "We both come with our own histories."

Kathy unrolled her silverware from the napkin. "Yes, but

I'm not interested in being involved in any love triangle here. If you're romantically involved with Lisa, you need to make a decision whether you want to be with her or me. I'm not going to hang around for a maybe."

Despite the insecurities she revealed earlier about the changes in her life, she was proud of the fact that she'd gone a few months without having a boyfriend. In the past, if she and Jeremy got in an argument or took a break—no matter how short—she went on dates with different men in an attempt to make Jeremy jealous and bring him back. It wasn't until she and Milo called it quits that she remained single for a significant period of time.

Jeremy nodded. "I get that. And I won't leave you hanging. I like being with you, Kathy. But we broke up for a reason. We need to figure out if that reason still exists."

"We will." She smiled. "But let's move on from that. We were getting to know each other again before you saw Lisa. Let's try to forget that she ever showed up."

"Sounds good to me. How's your food?"

As the conversation turned casual again, the thought of Lisa remained heavy on her mind. Kathy had been doing so well on her own until Samantha's wedding when Jeremy stumbled back into her life. Now she was potentially breaking up a relationship to revive an old one. How did she let herself get in this situation?

CHAPTER 6

The way Steven stabbed his steak told Samantha that he was still angry with her. After she had time to see it from his side, she couldn't blame him. They both wanted a fresh start. They just had different ways of seeing that fresh start.

Samantha set her fork down and pushed her salad aside. Despite the change in atmosphere and the time away from the apartment, Samantha could still smell the mix of paint and cigarettes. It was making her stomach queasy and she didn't trust it to keep anything down.

She looked across the table to her husband. He leaned against his fist and kept his eyes on his plate as he chewed. She needed to smooth things out with him because she didn't want this to turn into a huge argument. Discussing it in a public place where he would have to maintain any outbursts was a dirty move, but one she knew she'd use again and again throughout her marriage.

"I'm not saying no to the idea of having our own place." Samantha looked up at him, hoping that would be enough to get a response out of him. No such luck. "I just want to discuss it a bit before we make any changes. I want to do it when the time is right for us."

"So after our *wedding* isn't the right time for us?" he asked abruptly.

Samantha sighed, stuck for words. Again, he had a point. But she had her own, too. Where they currently lived was more than a house to her. It was her home. Her history. Her heritage. She was not about to throw that away so easily.

"Or is this your way of telling me that we're never going to come across the *right* time?" Steven asked. "Don't start manipulating me to get your way. That's not what I signed up for when I made those vows."

"Of course not," she said. "I'm not trying to manipulate you. I just don't think we're ready yet."

He waved his fork at her. "So tell me, besides me moving in and us wearing rings, what exactly has changed in the time since we've been married? How is our life now different from how it was when we were just dating?"

She shrugged. "I feel different being your wife instead of just your girlfriend. Like our relationship has a level of credibility it didn't quite have before."

Steven cut his steak into pieces. "Samantha, I looked forward to the changes we were going to make together. Getting our own place, figuring out our vibe as husband and wife, someday having kids and raising them. That's what I wanted with you. But now it just seems like I'm making the changes alone to fit the life that *you've* created. Like your life wouldn't change much if I wasn't here."

"Steven, of course that's not true," she said. "I never meant to make you feel that way."

"Well, you did." He took another bite.

"I just need time to adjust to the idea," she said. "Figure out what we want, what's going on with the house we live in now—I'm not going to sell it. That's not an option. So before we started looking for places for the two of us, I thought that we'd sit down with Kathy and make sure she could afford the house on her own. Or maybe she would decide to get her own place and we'd take the house. These are the conversations I thought we'd have before you scheduled an apartment tour for us without even telling me."

He sighed. "I thought it'd be a surprise."

"It definitely was," she said with the hint of a smile.

They studied each other, feeling the weight of the tension break down between them once they both aired what was on their mind. Still no solution, but heading in that direction.

"I was just blindsided because for the last couple months, I got the impression that you were moving *in*. That after the wedding, my house would become *our* house and that would be that."

"And I thought it was obvious that it was a temporary thing," Steven admitted. "I mean, I put most of my stuff in storage."

"That's a bill we both share now." Her smile quickly faded as her head began to throb.

"What's the matter?"

She shook her head. "Nothing, I just have a headache. I've been feeling off since this afternoon." *Since the showing.*

"Maybe you should eat something?"

"I don't think I'll be able to keep it down," she said.

He looked down at his plate, which was mostly cleared. "You should lay down. I'll get the check so we can go home."

CHAPTER 7

Scarlett stood between the aisles at Shea's and mimed her choreography on her own, trying to practice each step and make it natural. Like each movement was second-nature. The less she had to worry about dancing, the more she could focus on the few singing parts she had.

Singing wasn't her strength. She could carry a tune and she held her own—she was certainly improving—but she didn't have the natural set of pipes like the more prominent roles required.

"Do you want a mirror?" Oliver asked behind her suddenly.

She jumped and turned to face him, swatting at his arm in the process. "You did that on purpose!"

He laughed. "Can you blame me? You were right there! An

easy target!" He tried to pull her into a hug, but she pushed away from him playfully.

"No, you can't touch me!" she said between giggles. "Not after that!"

"So are you two dating now?" Ella called from across the stage. All the performers—and even some of the crew—were sitting throughout the stage eating sandwiches, salads, and whatever else they had for lunch.

All eyes turned to Scarlett and Oliver and they both straightened up at the attention.

"What?" Scarlett asked to buy time.

"I just find it funny how you say you don't date locals and yet here you are," she went on.

"Yeah," Marjorie said from beside Ella. "You used to be real strict about that."

It had been three days since Scarlett and Oliver first met. Two days since their not-a-date date, with only a week and a half remaining in Scarlett's stay in Buffalo. That kiss on the first outing had been the only one they'd shared so far. She wondered if there'd be more. They'd been flirty ever since they went to dinner, but nothing more than that.

As much as Scarlett liked Oliver and wanted to spend more time with him, she knew the girls were right. There was a reason she implemented the rule to begin with. What was going to happen when Scarlett and the rest of the production inevitably rolled out of town while Oliver stayed behind?

Nothing but heartbreak, that's what.

"So are you breaking your own rule?" Ella pushed.

Scarlett stared at her, forcing herself to meet Ella's eyes while also avoiding Oliver's. She tried to swallow to alleviate her sudden dry throat, but it didn't work. Finally, quietly, she said, "No, I'm not."

Ella set her sandwich down and got to her feet, hopping down from the stage and stepping toward Oliver. "Well then, if you're a free man, when are you going to take me out?"

"Uh, you're—I'm flattered by your interest, and you're obviously a very beautiful woman, but my eyes are set on Scarlett."

The room erupted in fits of laughter at Oliver's rejection, which made his cheeks flare up red. Scarlett couldn't help but smile at how cute he looked to be embarrassed.

"But Scarlett even said herself that she doesn't want to date you," she said.

He smiled. "Yeah, I know. She told me when I first met her and she still went out with me the other night." He shrugged. "People change."

Several people on the stage began clapping and hooting as Ella was denied a second time.

Jutting out her bottom jaw in anger, Ella huffed and stormed off backstage.

"I'm sorry," Scarlett murmured to Oliver, but he refused to look her in the eyes.

"I should probably go apologize to Ella," he said, then turned and followed her out.

Scarlett watched him go until he was out of sight, kicking herself for hurting him. But that was the very reason she came up with that rule. Pain was inevitable with relationships. Better to stay as far away from them as possible when she was incapable of maintaining one.

Taking a seat on the edge of the stage, Scarlett pulled out her lunch and began eating. She never felt so isolated as she did now and it was the first time she'd noticed that she was the only one who didn't have a clique of friends to hang out with. Sure, everyone was friendly with her, but given the option, everyone always chose other people over her.

It was probably the reason she was drawn to Oliver and the attention he gave her.

Not wanting to make it obvious that she was eating lunch alone—high school memories flashed in her mind—Scarlett decided to go and apologize to both Ella and Oliver. She needed to be the bigger person, especially with Oliver. She couldn't keep stringing him along if he had genuine feelings for her.

Scarlett stepped backstage and saw one of the doors leading out to the alley was propped open. She stepped through and saw Oliver and Ella locked in a kiss.

At the appearance of Scarlett, Oliver pulled away.

"It's not what it looks like!" he declared. "I was just telling

Ella that I'm not trying to send her mixed—" As if it were a compulsion, he turned and planted a kiss on Ella's lips again. Just as quickly as it happened, it ended. "—messages!"

"Then why are you kissing her?" Scarlett figured she might have a clue why, but she wasn't quite sure. She needed further proof.

Oliver kissed Ella again, who smiled and wrapped her arms around his neck. When he pulled away, he shrugged off her attempt at an embrace.

"I don't know!" he shouted.

"Looks like he's chosen me over you," Ella told her. "If you ask me, that's the right choice. I actually *want* him."

Scarlett had seen this sort of mischief before. Never quite so repetitive, but still, she'd seen it. Ella had had five minutes alone with Oliver, who had only come out here to apologize and now suddenly he was kissing her against his will?

A spell had been cast, which meant that Ella was a witch. If she were an enchantress like Scarlett, Oliver wouldn't kiss her unless that was his true heart's desire.

"Why don't you drop the charade and remove whatever you've put on him?" Scarlett said.

"I'm sure I don't know what you're talking about." Ella leaned forward and puckered her lips. As if on cue, Oliver turned and kissed her.

"Bull. You know exactly what I'm talking about."

Ella shrugged. "What are you going to do about it?"

Scarlett stepped toward Oliver and pulled him away from Ella.

"If there's anything you can do, please," he said. "I don't mean to keep kissing her."

"Shh." She placed her hands on his cheeks and muttered the incantation softly to herself.

Remove the magic influence,
to let this man control his kiss.

For a brief second, Oliver's eyes shone pink, before returning to normal. Scarlett looked into them and smiled.

"All better?"

He nodded. "I think so. How'd you do that?"

"Why don't you keep this our little secret?" she asked. "We can talk about it later."

Nervously, he nodded again. "I'll want answers."

Scarlett looked over at Ella, who stared in surprise. "You and me both." She turned back to Oliver. "Why don't you go back inside? I want to talk to Ella alone."

Oliver disappeared through the door and the two women studied each other.

Ella crossed her arms. "Looks like we were both keeping secrets."

"Except I don't use mine to manipulate innocent men."

"Oh please, like you didn't cast a spell on him!"

"I didn't! His attraction is genuine. My magic can't create it out of thin air, only push it along its natural path."

Ella stepped to the door. "Well, at least I know where your limitations are. Let the best woman win."

CHAPTER 8

From the kitchen, Kathy heard the familiar creak of the front door opening. Keys jangled as they were tossed on the table near the door where the mail and the rest of the knickknacks were thrown.

Kathy sat at the kitchen table, hunched over a heart-shaped box of cherry cordials, flipping through a copy of *Cosmopolitan*. Both of which she had picked up at the grocery store when she stopped to get milk on her way home from her awkward dinner date with Jeremy.

Without a word from the front of the house, Kathy heard the stairs creak as someone walked up—she guessed Steven by his heavy footsteps. A moment later, Samantha stepped into the kitchen.

"Hey," she said as she went straight to the stove and put on a kettle.

"Are you and Steven fighting?" Kathy bit into another chocolate, causing the cream filling to drip on her chin. She used her middle finger to swipe it up and licked it clean.

"No, not really. I don't think."

"Well, your silent entry, immediate separation, and rush to the stove say otherwise," Kathy pushed.

Samantha approached her. "Like you're one to talk. What is this?" She reached down and flipped the pages to see the cover. "*Cosmo*? Seriously?"

Kathy shrugged. "The headlines caught my attention."

Samantha scanned the titles: *How to Attract Men Like Crazy*; *Where the Good Men Are (Are There Jobs Too?)*; and *Closing the Deal (Marriage!)*. She raised an eyebrow and looked at her sister.

"Okay, fine, I didn't have a great night, either," Kathy admitted.

Samantha returned to the steaming kettle. "What happened?"

Kathy waved her finger at her big sister. "No, you first!"

"I don't want to talk about it right now."

Sighing, Kathy groaned. "*Fine*. Jeremy met up with me after class today and asked me to dinner."

"I thought you were keeping your distance?" Samantha filled a mug with hot water and reached for a box of tea bags.

"Well, I'm treading carefully, but we still need to see each other from time-to-time to see if there's anything left between us."

Samantha carried her mug over to the table and sat beside Kathy. "True."

"So anyway, we were chatting, catching up. Kind of awkward, but it's been months so what are you going to do?"

"Perhaps reconnect *before* you slip between the sheets again?"

"I *knew* I shouldn't have told you that!"

Samantha put up her hand in surrender. "Sorry. Go on."

Kathy reached for another cherry cordial. "I don't know if I want to. You've made it clear that you don't want me seeing him again."

"I'm nervous about it, that's all. I just don't want to see you get hurt. *And* I was a little annoyed that you ditched my wedding to get laid."

"I came back and helped clean up!"

Samantha gave her a look, then asked, "So what happened at dinner that made it not a great night?"

Kathy let out a heavy breath. "Jeremy apparently has been seeing other people since we broke up."

"So have you."

"Right, but Milo isn't the one who showed up at dinner tonight."

"Oh."

"Yeah."

"How was she?"

Kathy rolled her eyes and reached for another candy. "She seems perfectly nice, honestly. A little preppy, if you ask me, but I suppose I don't have a fair judgment of her." She dropped the candy and pushed away the box. "Have some of these, I've already had too much."

Samantha made a face and pushed them further away. "No thanks. So does this mean you and Jeremy are done? Again."

"Not necessarily." Kathy slid the cover on the box. "I don't know what the story is with this Lisa girl. He wouldn't be dating me if he was also dating her. And he and I didn't say we were *exclusive.*"

"Do you want to be exclusive?"

Kathy smoothed out the folded corner of the magazine. "I don't know."

"I think that's the first step before you expect anything from Jeremy and potentially break up another relationship."

"He just said she was a friend," Kathy added.

"And you tell him you don't have any magical powers. People don't usually say what they mean."

"True. I'll have to figure it out. But now's your turn. What happened tonight?"

Samantha took a careful sip of her tea. "Steven surprised me with a showing of a townhouse out near your school."

"A townhouse? Are you guys moving out?"

"No, we're not."

"Oh. I didn't realize you were considering it, though."

"*I* wasn't. He was. Or is."

"Ah."

Samantha took another sip. "Hence, the bad night."

"How did you react?"

"Not the best, actually. He was really excited about it and I kind of burst his bubble. I feel bad because he wants us to start a life together—and I do too—but this house…"

"Yeah, I know. I don't want to lose it either."

"Especially because we fought so hard to keep it," Samantha added.

"Did you tell him about the significance of this house?"

"Yeah. And I know he understands, but I'm not sure he entirely *gets* it, you know? Anyway, that's not even the biggest problem. He feels like I'm making decisions without him. We agreed to hold off moving out until we've weighed all of our options and discussed it but I can tell he's still disappointed."

Kathy made a face. "Sounds like we're both disappointing our men. Doesn't really add up to a happy Valentine's Day, does it?"

CHAPTER 9

Samantha parked herself in a chair at the conference table at Darius Wilcox, CPA. Her head was swimming. The tea the night before and the full night's sleep didn't do much to fight off whatever illness she was apparently succumbing to. She no longer thought it was from the funky smell of the apartment tour. It was winter, after all, so she must've caught something from somewhere. All she knew was she couldn't wait to get home and go to bed.

The rest of the room filled in. Mr. Marsden, Cliff, Jack, even Stacy from the front desk. It was their weekly staff meeting to keep everyone on the same page with operations related to the business and their clients.

"Are we all ready to get started?" Mr. Marsden asked.

"Samantha, honey, are you okay?" Stacy gave her a concerned look. If they were closer, Samantha thought that Stacy would've reached out and felt her forehead.

"Not great, but I'm here."

"Do you want to go home and rest?" Mr. Marsden asked. "We can fill you in on everything later."

"No, I'll be fine for the meeting," she said. "I'll take a half day and go home afterwards if that's okay."

"Of course it is!" Mr. Marsden said. "If you need to leave halfway through, just let me know."

Samantha smiled, appreciating the sentiment. At the same time, she hated being the center of attention for something beyond her control.

"All right, well, tax season is upon us." Mr. Marsden moved right into the meeting. "We're about to have an influx of work, a lot of calls have already started coming in. That means longer hours, overtime, and all of that. This is our time to shine. People are turning to us to help them make sense of what they've been screwing up all year."

Everyone chuckled except Samantha. She suddenly noticed Cliff's aftershave. He was sitting beside her and it seemed to be radiating throughout the room, challenged only by Jack's cigarette burning in his left hand. The smell reminded Samantha of the townhouse and suddenly her lightheadedness was met with nausea.

"It's a heavy lift for such a small team, but I have confidence that we can pull it off," Mr. Marsden continued. "While we handle that, however, we still need to maintain our regular clients and their portfolios."

Samantha was no longer listening. The room began to spin and she leaned in to her chair, bracing her hands against the arm rests. It was everything she could do to try to make her vision stop spinning.

She looks like she's going to pass out, Stacy's voice said in her head.

Maybe we should do something, Cliff thought.

How does Mr. Marsden not even see that Sam looks terrible? Stacy again.

She was losing control of her power. Losing control of everything. In a matter of seconds, she went from trying to regain control of her body to staring up at the ceiling as her coworkers hovered over her.

So much for no longer being the center of attention.

CHAPTER 10

- MARCH 1988 -

With eyes closed, Scarlett sat back in her seat on the balcony of Kleinhans Music Hall and enjoyed being among the audience for once. The music of the Buffalo Philharmonic Orchestra soothed her and made her date with Oliver even more special.

And she was finally allowing herself to admit it now: she was dating Oliver. It had been exactly one week since they met. They'd gone through a week's worth of rehearsals and one round of shows: Thursday's premiere, Friday's evening show, and two shows on Saturday. She had one final one coming up at the end of the week, but she wanted the week to stretch on forever, only so she could spend more time with Oliver.

As if he knew that she was thinking about him, Oliver

reached over and took Scarlett's hand. She opened her eyes and squeezed back, leaning in to him as they watched the concert play out before them beautifully.

After the spell Ella had cast on Oliver, Scarlett decided to ease up on her rule. It seemed so arbitrary in retrospect. Oliver was amazing, as she had come to find out over the last few days. So what if they didn't have a future? It didn't mean they couldn't enjoy the time they *did* have together.

And he'd made sure they maximized that time together. He'd shown her around the city—this stop at Kleinhans being the latest in the "Tour of Buffalo Extravaganza," as he called it. Oliver had taken her to formal dinners, cooked her dinner in his studio apartment, and they even made it back to that bar in Allentown after her show last night to dance some more. Since yesterday was also Saturday and she had two shows, he managed to squeeze in a date by taking her out to lunch before she had to get into costume for the matinée. She'd never met anyone who wanted to spend so much time with her.

After the orchestra hit the final crescendo and the audience erupted into applause, Oliver took Scarlett by the hand and led her back to the lobby before the crowd could fill in.

"That was beautiful," she told him. "I've never seen an orchestra perform. Thank you for bringing me!"

"I told you, I want you to see as much of this city as possible."

"Are you sure this isn't just a ploy to try to get me to stay?"

He shrugged. "Can't really blame me for trying, can you?"

"Of course not." She leaned forward and kissed him. They came so easy now that she had allowed herself to let her guard down. "What do you say we skip dinner and just go back to your place?"

He smiled, his cheeks rising, revealing the faintest dimples. "I'd like that, but there's something I want to tell you first."

"Hmm?" Scarlett could hear the applause die off and a few people escape the auditorium early, just as they had.

"I don't want this to come across as a manipulation or anything, but I want to be honest." He looked down and took a deep breath, before meeting her eyes again. "I think I'm falling in love with you."

Her mouth hung open and she instinctively pulled her hands away from his, as if she could flip the pencil over on their relationship to erase it and rewrite it. "Oliver, you don't really know me..."

"How can you say that?" He reached for her hands again and she let him take them. "We might not have known each other long, but I know a lot about you. For instance, I know you're...more than meets the eye."

After Ella had cast that spell on Oliver, forcing Scarlett to reverse it, her magic had been exposed to him. Fortunately, he hadn't asked any prying questions, even though she knew he had a lot of them. And she knew she could trust him with her secret.

Still, he deserved an explanation for what had happened and what he was getting into by getting closer to her. But it was a conversation she had managed to set aside for a bit. What was most surprising was that Oliver wasn't scared off by the unknown.

"I know you're guarded," he went on. "I know you try to keep people at arm's length to protect your heart. I know your parents live in Maine and you feel guilty for having left them, even though they're so proud and supportive of you. I know you wish you had a better singing voice or were a better dancer, even though I think you sound incredible and the way you move is something I dream about. I know you like pickles in your salad, but you're embarrassed to ask for it at restaurants. I know you have an obsession with antiques and a part of you wishes you had a big house to put them all in, but you wouldn't like staying in one place. It's only been a week, Scarlett, and so far I love everything about you. I know you and I know that I love you."

All throughout his speech, Scarlett couldn't help but smile. He was right. He knew a lot about her. And she knew so much about him, too. But was it love? Her magic allowed her to coax love to blossom, but it was always for other people. She'd never been in love herself, so how could she be sure that this was it? Shouldn't there be sparks and a sense of floating on air? Shouldn't it be obvious? Shouldn't it be simple and complicated all at the same time?

The truth was, though, she knew that she'd never felt this

way about anyone else.

"Well, I can tell you one thing." She interlocked her fingers with his. "I'm glad that I decided to break my own rule."

He leaned in and kissed her, but the moment was short-lived as the rest of the audience piled out of the auditorium, increasing the volume of the lobby with errant conversations.

"I think we better get out of here," he said. "You sure you want to skip dinner?"

"Definitely."

They joined hands and stepped out onto Pennsylvania Street.

"My apartment is maybe a fifteen minute walk from here," he said. "Is that okay?"

"Fine by me."

They talked more as they walked. Conversations that seemed to only strengthen Oliver's declaration. He told her how his mother used to take him and his sister to see the orchestra all the time, which is what got him interested in theater. He even tried out for several roles before realizing that he wasn't an actor—and he certainly wasn't a singer or dancer. Still, he loved being in the atmosphere of the large venues so he settled on working at Shea's instead.

He told her how his dream was to be a manager for the venue, working with other managers to bring shows into Shea's, and increasing the diversity of the shows while attracting all kinds of people to the theater. He wanted to bring it back to the popularity of its heyday.

Scarlett knew that their interest in old things was something they had in common. Something she loved about *him*. Maybe she felt stronger about his other attributes as well?

Oliver began walking up the stoop to his building and Scarlett paused out on the sidewalk and looked up and down Whitney Place.

"We're here already?" They had never come from the west before, always from downtown to the east. And usually in a cab.

He smirked. "It's not like they moved the building. Yes, this is where I live. You've been here before, haven't you? Or was that the other girl I've been seeing? It's so hard to keep track sometimes…"

She followed him through the door and swatted at his arm. "Not funny."

Up on the second floor, Oliver paused as he slipped the key into the lock. "You smell that?"

She leaned forward and sniffed. The scents of herbs came to her, but she couldn't quite place them. Maybe it was just a candle, but it was a very strong scent that told her the source was original, not manufactured. "Yeah, kind of like…incense or something."

He swung open the door and stopped. Ella sat on the floor in the middle of his apartment. There was a single yellow candle lit in front of her and smoking herbs in a pot pulled from Oliver's cupboard, all resting on an embroidered silk altar rug.

Ella was casting a spell.

Or had already done so. She murmured the words under her breath so quietly and so fast that Scarlett couldn't make them out.

Before she could really take in what Ella was doing, the witch extended her arm out toward Oliver. A dark shadow passed over him as her magic took hold.

"What did you do to him?" Scarlett stepped forward and blew out the candle, as if that tiny act would reverse Ella's magic.

"You'll see," she said as she rose to her feet. "I think I've been pretty generous sharing him with you up until now. I think for the rest of the week it'd be fair if you let me have him."

"He's not a *toy*, Ella. He can decide for himself who he wants to be with."

"Can he?"

Scarlett turned to Oliver for an answer, but he stared back at her with a blank expression.

"Oliver?" she asked quietly.

"I don't love you," he said in a monotone voice.

Even though Scarlett knew he wasn't saying those words of his own free will, they still hurt. Especially as she debated whether or not she loved him.

Turning to Ella, she said, "You need to take off that spell."

"Why should I?" Ella approached Oliver and grabbed his

chin to guide his gaze to her.

"Can't you just take rejection quietly like everyone else does?" Scarlett stepped toward the altar and searched through the herbs that Ella had brought with her. Galangal root, hibiscus, and orris root. All ingredients that were used for lust spells and other forms of manipulation.

Sticking her bare hand in the burning bundle of herbs, Scarlett did her best to pull away the hibiscus. Out of the bunch, it was the only one that didn't also have properties that protected people against black magic or negative energy.

Scarlett could use Ella's own altar to reverse her spell.

"What are you doing?" Ella asked. She stepped toward the altar, but Scarlett was faster with her own incantation.

Show this man's true dedication
and reverse the manipulation!
Let him speak of his own free will.
Follow his heart and break the spell.

A subtle glow came over Oliver as Scarlett's magic took hold. Both she and Ella stopped and stared at him, waiting to see if the spell had worked. If Ella's magic had been erased.

All the light seemed to have vanished from Oliver's eyes and he stared at Scarlett vacantly. She worried that they had cast too many spells on him in too short a time and it caused his brain to burn out and make him a zombie.

If something like that was even possible.

"Oliver?" she called. "Can you hear me?"

"Look what you did," Ella said. "You've ruined him!"

Scarlett kept her focus on Oliver. She rose to her feet and stepped toward him. "Oliver, I hope you can hear me because I need to tell you how much you mean to me. I'm sorry I didn't say it earlier when you did. I love you, Oliver. You were right; I was scared of getting my heart broken, but I realize now how stupid that sounds. I don't care if I'm leaving at the end of the week, all I want to be is with you." She leaned forward on her tiptoes and kissed him gently on the lips.

Ella groaned. "Oh, how touching. Like a spell like that is going to—" But her words stopped when she saw what was happening.

As Scarlett pulled away, Oliver blinked and sucked in a deep breath. "Scarlett! I was frozen! I couldn't talk, couldn't move, couldn't do anything!" He pulled her into a hug.

She squeezed him back as she felt a tear slip down her cheek.

"I'm sorry for what I said."

"It's not your fault." Scarlett turned to Ella. "She cast the spell on you."

"How were you able to reverse it?" Ella asked. "I thought you said your magic was only related to love?"

"Magic?" Oliver asked.

"And I love him!" Scarlett declared, bringing a smile to

Oliver's face. He kissed her again, apparently having forgotten the talk of magic.

"This isn't over, Scarlett." Ella stepped into the hallway and slammed the door behind her.

CHAPTER 11

Harriet Beecher Stowe and her role in the abolitionist movement.

Kathy tried her hardest to figure out the direction her essay would take for her Early American Literature class. She was at work, refolding clothes from display tables that had been destroyed by women who were in a desperate search for their size.

Refolding was a mindless activity and something Kathy always tried to use to help get her thoughts in order for her homework so she could hit the ground running when she actually had time to work on it.

Today, however, her efforts were coming up empty.

Harriet Beecher Stowe, best known for her book, Uncle Tom's

Cabin, *used her pen to highlight the horrors of slavery in the South…*

It was a great first line, but it was as far as she could get. She couldn't stop thinking about Jeremy and Lisa. How did they meet? Were they close? Did their conversations come easy? Did they have any awkward moments like Kathy was currently experiencing with him? Were they getting serious? Did Jeremy tell Lisa that he loved her? Did they sleep together already?

Kathy shook her head to wipe her thoughts away. She used the folding table to finish up folding a pair of acid-wash jeans with perfect creases to show off the product to potential buyers. After nearly six months of working in the mall, she'd perfected the art of folding, which wasn't a skill she was necessarily proud of. Definitely not résumé-worthy.

With that table all sorted and straightened, Kathy pushed the folding table through racks of clothes back toward the stock room. She stopped dead when she caught a glimpse of a familiar face.

Lisa stood only two racks over with her faux-leather purse slung over her shoulder. She studied a red and white blouse with puffy shoulder pads. Luckily, she hadn't spotted Kathy yet.

As the witch turned to maneuver away from the potentially humbling situation, the folding table caught on the leg of one of the clothes racks, causing hangers to clang together and several winter jackets to rustle loudly.

Lisa turned to the commotion. Kathy unhooked the leg of

the table and tried to push it free, but it was too late. She had been spotted.

"Excuse me? Do you need help?" Lisa stepped forward. One of the blouses from the racks was slung over her arm. When she met Kathy's eyes, her brow furrowed a bit. "You look familiar. Where do I know you from?"

The tiniest trickle of relief came to Kathy.

Maybe I can get out of this before she realizes who I am!

Kathy shrugged and pushed the folding table into the aisle, away from racks of clothes. Lisa followed her.

"I know! You're Jeremy's friend! Um…Kathy, right?"

Damn it. Now I'm stuck. Kathy turned and smiled. "Right! And you're…" She feigned forgetfulness.

"Lisa," she said with a beaming smile.

"That's it. Well, it was nice seeing—"

"You know, I couldn't help but wonder about last night," Lisa pressed on. "You and Jeremy, out to dinner. I don't mean to pry, but were you two…out on a date?"

Kathy's mouth went dry and she stammered for something to say. "Um…we were actually—"

"I know you two are old friends."

Kathy wanted to tell this woman that she and Jeremy were trying to figure out if they should get back together. It's what Lisa deserved to know if she was in any way romantically involved with Jeremy. But then, if that's the type of relationship Lisa and Jeremy had, then Kathy would be the one breaking them up if she got back together with him. If Jeremy was dating Lisa, she didn't want to destroy that relationship just for a maybe.

Offering a half-hearted smile, Kathy said, "Yes, we're just friends."

Lisa's smile seemed to brighten. "Oh! Okay!"

Now Kathy's heart was racing as she saw the happy expression on this woman's face that basically confirmed that there was another relationship blossoming. "Are you and Jeremy…?"

Lisa waved the air and distracted herself by inspecting the rack of winter coats Kathy had nearly taken out. "Oh, I don't know. I mean, *technically* nothing has been made official, but I'd say things are definitely heading in that direction."

While a polite smile spread across Kathy's face, her heart was simultaneously dropping into her stomach. Of course Jeremy was seeing Lisa. He had every right to. But ever since she and him had reconnected, she'd been building up hope that they were about to get back together. Now, she knew the noble thing was to stand down and let Jeremy and Lisa's relationship take off.

What hurt the most for Kathy was realizing that while she'd been keeping Jeremy at arm's length for the last three weeks, he'd been doing the same to her. Only, he was doing it because he was seeing someone else.

"Well, I've got to get back to work," Kathy said.

ENCHANTRESS

"It was nice talking to you!" Lisa beamed.

Kathy turned and pushed the table back to the stock room.

It was all she could do to keep herself from falling apart.

CHAPTER 12

- MARCH 1988 -

Despite the warm water cascading down her back, Scarlett still felt like her muscles were tight with stress. She tried to get the incident with Ella the night before out of her mind, but Oliver naturally had questions. And she'd put him off long enough. So now, on top of worrying about what Ella might do, she debated how best to approach the conversation with the new love of her life—that declaration in itself was yet another thing to stress about.

"Morning," Oliver said on the other side of the shower curtain.

She could hear him pull his toothbrush from the cup by the sink.

"Morning," she replied with almost no enthusiasm.

Oliver apparently didn't pick up on that. "So you're an enchantress?"

She'd told him that much last night, but put off any other questions. "Mm-hmm."

"Is that like a witch?"

Scarlett sighed and reached for the bar of soap perched on a plastic clip of the claw-foot tub. Oliver's apartment was in an old building that was built at a time when features like these were common. She loved the idea of it, but she also would be lying if she said she wasn't grossed out by the tub a bit. It had been neglected over the decades and needed some serious T.L.C. to get it back up to snuff.

"Not exactly like a witch," she explained. "Although we're similar." She was amazed at how casual this conversation was, talking through their morning routine. Like a couple discussing what they needed from the grocery store. "We can only do magic related to love."

"Like Cupid?"

She laughed. "No quite as extravagant as that fairy tale. Honestly, I don't really use my magic much. Sometimes I'll play matchmaker for a couple who obviously wants to be together. Just a simple incantation or a potion and they finally give in to their desires. But it has to be genuine. I can't create it out of thin air."

"Did you use your magic on us?"

"I've never used my magic on my own love life." She stepped

back into the water and rinsed one final time. "I don't know if it'd even work."

"Hmm. Interesting."

"Trust me, even though this past week has been a whirlwind, everything is true."

"That's reassuring, but I have another question."

"Shoot." Scarlett slowly increased the level of hot water to near-scalding. She'd regret it when she got out of the shower and was surrounded by steam, but for now it was just starting to help her relax.

"If you're an enchantress, what does that make Ella? She was able to cast a spell on me, but you were able to undo it. Enchantresses must be pretty strong then, right?"

Again, Scarlett laughed. "Hardly. And that was two questions."

She heard him spit, then say, "Sue me."

"Enchantresses are only superior with magic related to love," she explained. "So I think Ella must be a witch. The spells she cast had to do with love—or rather, a manipulation of love—but they weren't very successful and I was able to break them pretty easily. Either she's a witch or she's a terrible enchantress gone rogue."

"So if she's a witch, she could try other magic to keep us apart, right?"

"Let's hope she doesn't."

His pause was poignant. Scarlett could tell he was thinking

things over thoroughly in his head.

"I think we should run away," he said. "Get as far away from her as possible to keep her from casting anymore spells."

"Oliver, I'm not going to live in fear my whole life. Besides, I can handle Ella." Deciding she'd been in the shower long enough, she reached down and turned off the water. After grabbing a towel from the hook and wrapping it around herself, she slid open the curtain.

Oliver leaned against the vanity, staring at the floor with a stern expression.

"What's the matter?"

He breathed in a deep breath and slowly turned to look at her. "Your show is only in town for a few more days. What are we going to do after that?"

"Well, you could always join me on tour. Be a roadie or something."

Before she even finished, he began shaking his head. "My life is here in Buffalo. I don't want to uproot it."

"You were the one who just suggested we run away together."

"Only to get away from Ella!"

Scarlett snapped her mouth shut to keep in any snarky replies. Arguing with each other was not how she wanted to spend their last few days. Maybe an opportunity would turn up before she needed to leave. Doubtful, but she could hope.

Fishing in the pocket of his jeans, he pulled out the pocket knife he always carried with him and handed it to her. "Here."

"What's this for?" she asked.

"I want you to always be prepared, even when I'm not with you."

She tried to give it back to him, but he refused. "Oliver—"

"No, I want you to have it. If, for no other reason than to remember me by."

"We're not going any—" She stopped herself. She couldn't promise that she'd always be around because she wasn't sure that was the case. Finally, she said, "Thank you."

Oliver nodded. Quietly, he said, "I see now why you don't date locals."

CHAPTER 13

After Kathy's conversation with Lisa, she hadn't felt like herself at all. Ever since Lisa left the store, Kathy had been trying her best to occupy herself. She finished up the back stock, worked the register for a bit, and even did some more straightening until her manager told her to go on break.

As Kathy stepped into the concourse and smelled the tasty scents wafting up from the food court around the corner, she realized just how hungry she was. Perhaps filling her stomach would help her feel better.

"Excuse me, miss!" Kathy turned in her pursuit of lunch and looked around. In the middle of the concourse, among the carts selling sunglasses, cheap jewelry, and other knickknacks, sat a woman behind a table with a black tablecloth draped over it.

The woman had curly red hair, a flowing green dress that shimmered in the light, and bright red lips. As the two women made eye contact, the red-haired woman beckoned Kathy closer with a wave of her hand.

Kathy looked forlornly down the food court, but figured an extra five minutes couldn't hurt. Besides, with a getup like this, she was dying to know just what this woman wanted. Although, truth be told, she and her sister had seen weirder.

"Can I help—" Kathy started, but the woman cut her off with an aggressive whisper.

"I noticed a dark energy in your aura!"

Rolling her eyes, Kathy crossed her arms. That was one of the oldest tricks in the book for mall psychics like this. Tell someone they're in grave danger or some other way to make them paranoid and pay for an *authentic* reading. As if this woman had any ounce of magical energy in her veins at all.

"What troubles you, dear?" the woman asked.

"Right now it's my empty stomach." Kathy turned to leave, but the woman called to her.

"Wait! Whatever's troubling you is much greater than physical nourishment." She patted her chest. "Something is troubling your soul."

Kathy eyed her, reluctantly curious. The state of her relationship with Jeremy *was* bothering her deep down, but again, this woman's declarations were so vague that they could be applied to anyone.

"You are hesitant, I can see that, but I also sense belief in your mind," the woman pressed. "You have had experience with the magical arts before."

At the mention of magic, Kathy took a seat and looked around to see if anyone had picked up on the use of the word. The mall was steady, although not too terribly packed being that it was the middle of the day on Thursday. Still, she thought it best to sit and act like they were having a friendly conversation than stand over the woman and draw more attention to them.

"Why do you say that?" Kathy asked.

"So it's true."

"I don't know what you're trying to accuse me of, but—"

The woman put up her hands in surrender and Kathy noticed her fingers were adorned with jeweled rings and bracelets that clanged together whenever she moved her arms. "No accusations here," the woman said. "I'm only trying to help. Now, even if you don't believe that I can *magically* help you, I think we can both agree that you have something on your mind, yes?"

Kathy licked her lips and sighed before nodding. No sense in denying it to a complete stranger.

"Now, you can stew in this misery all day or you can get it off your chest to a pair of listening ears. How's that sound?"

Just talking wouldn't hurt anyone, Kathy decided. Besides, she wanted to talk about it without worry of gossip from her coworkers or judgment from her sister. This stranger in the mall seemed like the perfect solution.

"Well, I used to date this guy, Jeremy," Kathy started. "We broke up last summer. His friend had died and he was under a lot of stress, plus he had to move in with me for a while for…reasons. It put a huge strain on an already crumbling relationship as we both drifted apart."

The woman sat patiently and nodded to show she was listening, but offered no other input so as to allow Kathy to continue. She didn't look bored or annoyed, which made Kathy wonder why she even cared. Still, it was nice to talk out loud about the things that had been rattling around in her head for weeks.

"Anyway, my sister got married last month and I ran into Jeremy again. It was a surprise to see him and we…hooked up." She glanced at the redheaded woman for a reaction, but there was none. "After that, I thought it was best if we took things slow because I did miss him and it was great being with him again, but we've both changed a lot since last summer. He's working full-time now, I'm going to school, and I work here…anyway, we're just different people than we were so I thought it might work out this time."

"But?"

Kathy swallowed to try to get rid of the lump forming in her throat. She hadn't cried yet today and she wasn't about to lose it with a fake psychic in the middle of the mall.

"Last night I found out he's been seeing someone else since we broke up," she said. "And I don't want to interfere with that relationship unless I know that Jeremy and I are going to work out this time. I'm just not sure that's the case. We haven't had a chance to really talk about the reasons we broke up in the first place. So…that's where I'm at."

The woman tapped a jeweled finger to her red lips. "Do you love him?"

Kathy sighed. "I thought I did, but…" *But a siren's magic had no effect on Jeremy because we weren't in love*, she thought to herself. Instead, she shrugged for the woman's benefit. "I'm not sure Jeremy ever loved me either."

The woman shook her head. "No. If a man says he loves you once and *shows* it, even if for only a short period of time, it means the love was true. However, he may have only been saying it out of habit after you both slowly fell out of love with one another. As you said, people change. They grow. Relationships fall apart if they're not worked on. These things happen."

"So what am I supposed to do now?"

"First," the woman held up a finger, "figure out if you're still in love with him. Second,"—another finger went up—"figure out if he's still in love with you."

"But how am I supposed to do that if he's seeing someone else?"

The woman smiled. "You're a witch and you don't know

how to determine if a man loves you?"

Kathy's jaw dropped. How did the woman know that? She had been careful not to make any mention of magic or her knowledge of its existence. Kathy's mind flashed to the exposure she reversed only a few weeks ago and the torment and scrutiny that came with it. She was not about to make that a reality again.

The woman seemed to recognize her own mistake. "That's not—you shouldn't worry. I didn't mean—"

Kathy got to her feet and retreated back toward the shop where she worked. "I—I have to go." She collided into people, who gave her dirty looks for being rude. Kathy didn't care. Her instincts told her to retreat and that's what she was doing. She didn't want to be exposed again.

She feared that it might already be too late.

CHAPTER 14

- MARCH 1988 -

Oliver stood offstage and watched as Scarlett and the rest of the dancers rehearsed for their next show later that night. They only had three more shows and then they were on the road again to the next city. The two weeks had flown by, the second having been shadowed in worry over the inevitable ending.

"All right, let's take a ten minute break," the director called out. "Get something to drink. We'll start work on Act II, Scene Three next."

Scarlett moved over to the edge of the stage where she had set her water bottle. Oliver stepped back further into the array of curtains. Better to start keeping their distance, let their love begin to wilt before it was immediately ripped from their lives.

He thought it might be better if he had some control over it. Maybe then it wouldn't hurt so bad when Scarlett rolled out of town.

How did he let himself get so swept up in her?

"Can somebody help me, please!" a woman called out from behind him.

Looking for a reason to seem busy, Oliver jumped at the opportunity and followed the direction he heard the voice.

"What do you need?" He stepped into the dark rehearsal room, where the door slammed shut behind him. Whirling around, he tried to see who was in there with him but the sudden darkness prevented him from making out anything other than shadows. "Hello? Who's here?"

Calling the power of present and past,
Seal this man in the hourglass.

Suddenly, the room burst into light as Ella's magic took hold. Oliver felt the room spinning as he was pulled toward Ella, who suddenly appeared by the door in the supernatural light.

In the next instant, he found himself sanding in a pit of sand, with more raining down on him. He spun around, quickly losing his balance in the sand, and falling on his butt. Undeterred, he looked around as the world around him seemed to move and light returned.

Ella.

He repeated the last words he had heard and figured she must've cast a spell that Scarlett wouldn't be able to break. Something unrelated to love. Something where Ella had the magical advantage.

Through the warped glass, he saw Ella's face peer in to look at him—large now that he was so small. She gave the hourglass a shake that sent Oliver's head spinning as he slid among the sand.

"In a few days, Scarlett will think you stayed behind in Buffalo and I can have you to myself."

Just as quickly as the light came, it was gone, accompanied with more shaking as she stuffed the hourglass away.

When his world finally stopped spinning and Oliver was left in total darkness, he worried if Scarlett would notice he was gone. If she would come looking for him. Or if she would assume his absence was a way to cope with their doomed relationship.

And if she did notice he was gone, would she even find him? Could she even free him if her powers only worked on magic related to love?

Maybe, he feared, he would be locked away in Ella's hourglass forever.

CHAPTER 15

From her perch on the couch underneath a warm blanket and snuggled between fluffy couch cushions, Samantha heard the phone ring. She debated letting it go until the answering machine got it, but figured it might be someone from work calling to check up on her. After her episode at that morning's meeting, she didn't need any of her co-workers reading into her silence and rushing over to rescue her.

Throwing the blanket back, she got to her feet and hurried to the kitchen to answer the phone. She grabbed it right at the last ring.

"Hello?"

"It's me," Steven said on the other end.

Samantha glanced at the clock on the wall and saw it was

just after twelve. He usually called her on her lunch break to chat. "Hi."

"Are you okay? I called your office and they said you went home sick."

She stretched the cord to the kitchen table and plopped down. It wasn't as comfortable as the warm couch, but it was better than standing. "I feel better now that I've had some rest. I think I just didn't have enough to eat last night or this morning and I just had low blood sugar. I ate something when I got home and I was able to keep it down, so that's good."

"That's a pretty low bar to set as a standard," he said.

"I know, but I only want to take this afternoon off at the most. I have a pile of work I need to get to." *Plus,* she added in her own head, *passing out in front of everyone was absolutely mortifying. Better to go in tomorrow all better so everyone can forget the whole thing ever happened.*

"Don't push it, Sam," he said. "If you're sick, let your body rest up and heal."

"It's only one day and then it's the weekend," Samantha said. "We'll see how I feel. Anyway, what's up? How's work?"

"It's okay, but I can't stop thinking about last night. I feel like we haven't been listening to each other about this townhouse."

I think it's more that we haven't been giving each other the answers we want to hear, Samantha thought, but decided it was best not to start an argument.

"I know your house is special to you," he went on, "and I

understand not wanting it to fall out of the family's hands, but Kathy's had a steady job for months now and could probably handle the bills on her own. And she's going to school. Soon she'll have a better job and then she'll be even better off. I just think it's a good idea for the two of us to have a clean slate and really mark the start of our life together by moving someplace new."

"Steven, I know where you're coming from, but from my perspective, this all came out of nowhere," she said. "We haven't even talked much about getting our own place and suddenly I'm touring a bland townhouse."

"I know. And I'm sorry for springing it on you like that. I just saw the ad in the paper and didn't want to pass up what could be a good opportunity. And honestly, I can see how the townhouse wasn't a perfect fit for us, but that doesn't mean we need to throw out the whole idea of getting our own place. Maybe something else. Something in a more traditional neighborhood. Maybe something not far from where we live now."

Samantha scoffed. The houses in their neighborhood were just as old as hers. They were either incredibly expensive or were held on to with an iron grip, much like Samantha was trying to do with hers. The newest neighbors on the street were Mr. and Mrs. Kors, directly across the street from them. And that was only because the house was significantly discounted after a shapeshifter killed the owners and committed even more murders in that house.

The specifics didn't make it into the news, but the murders weren't exactly marketing pieces.

"So that's just the end of the story?" Steven's voice grew in anger. "Just like that? You say no and that's how it is?"

She sighed. "I'm not trying to be dismissive, but I don't think you quite grasp how important this house is to me. It's been in our family for generations and—"

"I know that and it will continue to be with Kathy and her future kids, but—"

"When my dad disappeared, Kathy and I worked our asses off to keep it," Samantha pushed. "I'm talking two part-time jobs each on top of schoolwork and trying to stay under the radar of CPS until Kathy turned eighteen. It was incredibly stressful and difficult, but we did it. We managed. One of my biggest fears was that I would disappoint my whole family by being the one who couldn't keep the house that we've lived in for years and years. But we did it. And our reward for that suffering is maintaining the legacy of this house. I can't just throw away all of that hard work I put in just for a clean slate. This house has seen generations of families come and go, why can't we have our clean start here?"

He sighed on the other end. "I can understand that."

Samantha felt relief that he wasn't being dismissive of her in retaliation. Still, there was something in his voice that said that he wasn't completely satisfied with the outcome. "You still sound mad."

"Well, I'm not *happy*," he admitted. "But I understand your point. I guess I should've thought of that when I decided to marry a witch."

"To be fair, you wanted to marry me *before* you knew I was a witch," she said. "But I did give you that out in case you freaked. Now we're almost three weeks into this so-called happily-ever-after and you're stuck."

He chuckled. "You bet I am. Anyway, I guess I'll drop the whole moving out thing unless something *really* great comes along and even then, I'll talk to you before doing anything."

"Thanks."

"I'm going to get back to work. I'm glad you're feeling better. Rest up because I know you're going to work tomorrow regardless of what anyone says."

She smiled because she had already decided that. The only reason she left work today was because the rest of the office wanted her to go to the ER. Laying at home was the better option out of the two.

"I will. Love you."

"Love you too."

Samantha stood to return the phone to its cradle, then walked to the plastic bag sitting on the counter. She had stopped at the drug store on her way home and picked up a few things to try to help with her mysterious ailment in case her natural and magical remedies had no effect.

Pulling out the pink box, Samantha studied the pregnancy

test and wondered if she should actually take it. Did she really think she was pregnant or was the idea simply in her head because of expectations?

First comes love, then comes marriage, then comes baby in the baby carriage...

CHAPTER 16

- MARCH 1988 -

Scarlett shivered in the cold outside the backstage door. She hadn't seen Oliver during the show, but it was always such a madhouse during performances that it was entirely possible that they'd bypassed each other without even noticing. When she was working, she was in the zone, completely oblivious to the surroundings that didn't immediately require her attention.

One-by-one, Scarlett watched as the cast and the crew exited the venue and walked back to their hotel. At the sight of the director, Scarlett decided it was time to ask about Oliver. She didn't think he'd go home without saying anything to her, even if things had been off between them since their talk the other morning.

"Have you seen Oliver?" she asked him.

"Who?"

"Oliver, he's a stagehand. He works for Shea's."

The director shrugged. "Sorry, Scarlett. I don't know who he is by name. You could ask the manager, but I think he's gone home already."

Scarlett nodded. "Well, thanks anyway." She waved goodbye to him and peered in the door to the venue again. Maybe she should go look for Oliver, see if he got tied up talking to someone.

But how would that look if she had ignored him all day only to search him out at the end of the night when she wanted someone to hold? She'd grown accustomed to having a sleeping partner.

The next person through the door was Ella. Scarlett quickly rearranged her face so as to hide any worry.

Too late. Ella must've noticed something was bothering her and decided to take advantage.

"Oliver went home," she said bluntly. "He said he didn't want to wait for you because you were about to ditch him when we leave on Saturday."

Scarlett sidestepped the dig that was very clearly a lie. Oliver might be upset at the end of their relationship, but he wouldn't suddenly turn bitter. Still, she couldn't deny that he might've left without saying goodbye to try to resume his sense of normal. The life he had had before she came into his life.

"Okay, thank you," Scarlett said politely. It was best not to give Ella anything to respond to.

"Maybe next time you decide to date a local, you'll be able to better hold on to him."

"Hmm. Maybe." Turning, Scarlett started in the direction toward Whitney Place. To Oliver's apartment.

Their relationship might be coming to an end, but they still had two days and she wanted to spend it with him. At the very least, she wanted to *talk* about things.

By time she got to his apartment, her face was nearly numb from walking in the wind. She'd forgotten quite how far of a walk it was. Seemed even longer without anyone to keep her company.

Up on the second floor, she tried the door to his apartment, but it was locked. No surprise. She knocked twice.

"Oliver, it's me. Open up."

Nothing. Not even the sound of floorboards creaking on the other side.

She checked her watch. It was late. He might've gone right to bed. She knocked again, harder this time.

"Oliver! Let me in!"

Still nothing, and now she was getting annoyed at how childish he was being. Was he really just going to ignore her like this? She pounded on the door with her fist, which sent the neighboring door swinging open.

An old woman with curlers in her hair stuck her head out

the door. "Would you knock it off! He's not even home!"

"He isn't?"

"No. He usually brings up the mail for me at the end of the day, but he hasn't dropped it off yet. I have a hard time with stairs."

"Are you sure?"

"Sure as I see you standing there, although it is late and I *could* be dreaming…"

The only reason Scarlett thought Oliver was here was because of what Ella had told her. As if Ella had ever been truthful to her before.

Scarlett's eyes grew wide. Ella had casted spells on Oliver before. Maybe she had this time too. Maybe this time it was something that Scarlett couldn't reverse.

CHAPTER 17

See you on Monday!" Kathy called to her manager as she walked out of the store.

It was the end of the night and as she walked through the mall, the gates from all the storefronts were closing down around her. Kathy had agreed to stay for a double shift so that she could avoid running into that weird psychic lady who had called her out as a witch.

All day long, Kathy had been trying to figure out how she could've guessed that she was a witch. Kathy hadn't used her power in weeks, nor had she even cast any spells. Ever since Samantha's wedding, things had been very quiet on the magical front.

Until today.

Digging her hands in her winter coat, she made her way to her usual exit, bracing herself for the winter cold and the long walk across the enormous parking lot toward the death trap they called Route 19. It was the closest bus stop for her ride toward her house. She hadn't minded the trek in the fall when it was still decently warm, but navigating the snow, ice, and slush was no fun.

Still, her mind was consumed with the possibilities of how she had managed to expose her magic. Again. She supposed that she might've done something subconsciously with the amount of stress she was under with school and work, but she'd been under worse stresses before and hadn't performed any magic unknowingly.

And if that were the case, why hadn't anyone else noticed? The psychic was sitting out in the open concourse when Kathy saw her at lunch. If she was doing something magical, surely the rest of the crowd would've seen too.

Kathy tried to assure herself that this exposure would be nothing like the last one. Even if that psychic lady somehow knew her secret, there was no way she had proof like Steven's mother did in the alternate timeline that had been corrected prior to Samantha's wedding.

With the night sky in sight, Kathy pushed through the doors into the vestibule and let out a shriek when she spotted the psychic lady standing in wait.

"There you are!" the redhead said. "I've been waiting for you for the last hour!"

"Are you stalking me?" Kathy considered making a run for it out the door, but the woman would easily be able to catch up with her. It's not like Kathy was running to a car where she might be able to lose the psychic. She was on foot. Evenly matched.

"My name is Scarlett," the woman said. The mystique in her voice faded, replaced instead with a more casual, modern tone. "I apologize for scaring you off."

"Apology accepted." Kathy said quickly, then turned to the door. "I need to catch my bus." She winced as a cold breeze whipped across her face. It lasted only a second, but sent a chill to her bones that she knew she wouldn't be able to shake until she was in the warmth of her own house.

Scarlett followed behind her, pulling her own puffy coat around her shoulders. Her green flowing dress blew in the wind. "I'm not really a fortune teller."

"I figured that much." They meandered between snow-covered cars and huge piles created by the plows.

"I'm an enchantress," Scarlett continued. "I'm like a witch too, except that my magic—"

"Is related to love," Kathy said. "I know what an enchantress is." She scoffed. "If you ask me, magic cannot accurately have any kind of effect on love."

"That may be true when tried by inexperienced practitioners in magic related to love, such as yourself or any other witch, however, magic can reveal a lot about love without actively influencing it."

Another brisk gust blew through them. Kathy felt like her ears were going to fall off. She should've grabbed a headband when she left the house earlier.

"I need to get home," she said. "I don't want you to follow me the whole way."

They came up to a row of outlying buildings in the Millcreek Mall development, which helped block some of the wind blowing from the lake.

"Wait." Scarlett reached for Kathy's arm to stop her. "I'm sorry for scaring you earlier, but I was excited that I found a witch. I need your help."

Kathy studied her, trying to determine if the enchantress was being honest. It was in her nature as a witch to help people, but she wasn't about to be duped, either.

"In return, I will help you with your problem," Scarlett said.

"What problem?"

"The one you discussed earlier with me," she said. "About Jeremy."

Kathy wished she hadn't revealed that much to a perfect stranger. But then, she never thought the woman she was unloading all of her secrets to would end up being someone she would need to work with.

"What do you need help with?" The cold was wearing on Kathy's patience.

"It's not for me," Scarlett said. "It's for someone I love."

"If it's love you need help with, you're the enchantress, not me." Kathy turned to leave, but again Scarlett reached for her.

"No, wait!" she called out desperately. She stared into Kathy's eyes, heartbreak and anguish within them. "Please."

Kathy studied her a moment longer. Samantha wouldn't like inviting a problem into their lives, but then again, she also wouldn't like turning away someone who genuinely needed help. If nothing else, they needed to hear Scarlett out. Better to do it someplace warm and protected than out in the open like this.

"Fine," she said. "But the bus we need to catch will be here in about five minutes. Let's go."

CHAPTER 18

- MARCH 1988 -

Ella stood in the doorway to her hotel room when Scarlett came around the corner from the elevator. She was talking to another girl, who took one look at Scarlett and retreated back to her own room. Ella, meanwhile, remained propped up against the doorframe with a smug grin.

"What the hell did you do with Oliver?" Scarlett demanded.

"Did you misplace him?" She giggled and added, "To quote your exact words when I said I was interested in him: 'Be my guest.' I just took your advice."

Nancy, Ella's roommate, stepped into the doorway. "What's going on?"

"Scarlett, here, thinks I'm hiding that stagehand," Ella said. "Oliver. You remember him, right? The one she claims she's not dating but flirts with all the time. Scarlett practically bit my head off when I said I liked him."

"Don't pretend like you're innocent in this," Scarlett said. "I know you did something to him because you've tried before. Now I'm asking you again: what did you do to him?"

"I didn't do anything *to* him," Ella insisted. "I've been at work all day and then I came straight here. When did I have the chance?"

Nancy nodded. "It's true. We walked back to the hotel together and picked up something from the deli on Chippewa."

Scarlett herself remembered seeing Ella alone outside the theater, but the story still didn't add up. "Where is he? I went to his apartment and he's not there and he's not at the venue."

"He's gone, Scarlett," Ella said.

Despite her natural response to take everything Ella said with a grain of salt, Scarlett couldn't help but hear Oliver's own, magically-aided words ring in her head: *I don't love you.*

Obviously, that was just a spell, but it still hurt. Still left an impact on her. Maybe the past week and a half had had a bigger impact on Oliver. So much so that he needed to get away from all the memories of their love. Disappear long enough for Scarlett to leave his life forever.

Unless he was threatened. Maybe Ella realized that Scarlett would see through any spell cast on Oliver so she decided to threaten him with a spell she might cast on Scarlett. Without knowing much about magic, Oliver might've fallen for it. He might've left town just to protect Scarlett.

"I have to go." Turning, Scarlett jogged down the hall back to her own hotel room. Throwing the few items she had into her bag, she packed it all in.

Ever since she had arrived in Buffalo, so much had changed. *She* had changed. Once scared to leave the life she knew and settle down somewhere, Scarlett was now more scared of losing the person she cared for the most in the world.

Two doors down from her own was the director's hotel room. She was going to tell him she was quitting the show. And she wouldn't let him talk her out of it.

Sometimes, it was better to take risks than to play it safe.

Sometimes, some things are more important than job commitments.

Somewhere, Oliver was out there trying his best to avoid her.

And she needed to find him.

CHAPTER 19

The fire crackled in the fireplace as Samantha and Steven cozied up under a blanket on the couch. The TV wasn't on, they weren't reading anything, or even talking. They were just laying together, his arms wrapped around her from behind. Samantha knew it was Steven's way of trying to comfort her.

On the table beside the couch was the empty mug from Samantha's tea. She'd mixed in cinnamon to help balance out her blood sugar. Plus, it was tasty. After she drank it, she did feel a little better, although that was around the time that Steven came home from work and they'd been on the couch ever since.

"I should probably get you something to eat," he said, breaking their peaceful quiet.

She snuggled closer against him. "Five more minutes."

He wrapped his arms tighter around her.

They had sort of made up over the phone, but she could still sense his disappointment that their living situation wasn't going to change. She would've tried to make it up to him—probably could've cooked him dinner—if she was feeling better. But the way he came home and immediately tended to her told her that he just needed time to accept that things weren't going to change anytime soon.

Samantha felt herself begin to drift off to sleep when the front door burst open. Steven sat up, disrupting the perfect cocoon that they had made on the couch.

"Sam!" Kathy called out, but stopped short when she saw her sister in the living room. "Oh, sorry. Did I interrupt something?"

Samantha sat up and ran her hands through her matted hair. "Just resting."

Behind Kathy, a curly-haired redhead stepped into the doorway of the living room.

"Are you sick?" Kathy asked.

"I'm fine. Who's this?" By asking the question, Samantha tried to mask her annoyance that her peaceful evening had just been interrupted.

"This is Scarlett. She's an enchantress."

At that, Steven got to his feet. "I'll give you guys a minute."

Samantha reached for his hand, a last-ditch effort to will away the magical problem she knew was about to invade their lives and consume them for a short while.

"I'm just going to go start dinner," he said. "You stay here and take care of what you need to take care of."

"Is he mad?" Kathy asked in a soft voice. She took a seat in one of the chairs and motioned for Scarlett to take the other one. "Are you sure we didn't walk in on something?"

Samantha rolled her eyes. "He's fine. What's going on?"

"You need to hear Scarlett's story," Kathy said. "And keep an open mind. I was skeptical at first, but she explained it all to me on the way home and it sounds like something we need to help her with. It's heartbreaking."

"Wait a minute. Back up. Where did you meet her?"

Scarlett leaned forward. "I was working at the Millcreek Mall, acting as a fortune teller."

Samantha hooked an eyebrow, then gave her sister a look. "A fortune teller?"

"Sam, before you rush to judgment like I did, just hear her out," Kathy pleaded. "She needs our help."

Tucking her hair behind her ears, Samantha leaned back on the couch and looked to Scarlett.

"I'm not even sure where to start…"

"Start from the beginning," Kathy suggested. "She needs to hear it all, like you told me."

Scarlett sucked in her lips as she searched for the words. "Well, I used to be a performer on a traveling Broadway show. *Me and My Girl*, perhaps you've heard of it?"

Samantha nodded. "Are you playing at the Warner Theatre downtown?"

The enchantress shook her head. "No, I quit the show about a year ago. We were in Buffalo when I met Oliver. He was one of the crew workers for the venue. Up until I met him, I had a rule that I wouldn't get involved with anyone from the different cities we visited, but there was no denying the connection we developed almost immediately."

Samantha narrowed her eyes, unsure of how a romance had anything to do with their job as witches. Still, she decided to hear Scarlett out. She knew that if she didn't, she'd always wonder if they could've helped Scarlett. One of the curses of being a witch.

"On the show, there was another actress, Ella, who was very obviously jealous of the blossoming relationship I had with Oliver," Scarlett continued. "She tried the typical bullying tactics to interfere with our love, but when we continued to see each other, her torment advanced to magical intervention."

At this, Samantha perked up. "Was she another enchantress?"

Scarlett shook her head. "She's a witch. And a dark one, at that. She tried numerous spells on him to destroy our love, but her magic was unable to have a permanent effect on love. Only an enchantress's magic can, and even that is limited. Every spell that Ella cast, I was able to reverse because they were all related to love. But then she caught on. And she changed her tactic."

Samantha could tell that Scarlett was being honest. The emotion in her voice mixed with her determination was not something that could be easily mimicked. "What did Ella do?"

"A few days before our show was due to leave town, Oliver disappeared. I searched for him at the venue and his apartment, but nobody had seen him. I knew then that Ella was responsible and I confronted her. She claimed she had nothing to do with his disappearance, but I know differently. My thoughts were that she sent him somewhere, so I went out to find him."

"And I take it you haven't yet?" Samantha asked, even though she knew what the answer was.

"No, I haven't. Reality very quickly caught up to me. I had to pay for a place to stay, food to eat. Then I had to get jobs, all while keeping my eye open for where Oliver could be. I thought that after I left, Ella would've brought him back so she could have him. I tried to follow the show's tour route as best I could, but they had the resources to travel faster than I could. I did meet up with them in Indianapolis, but I had burned my bridges with the manager of the show and he wouldn't let me backstage. Even when I was able to confront Ella out on the street, she refused to tell me what happened to him. And now that it's been almost a year, I'm afraid that the effects of her spell will become permanent if I don't reverse it and find him."

As Scarlett wiped away tears, Kathy moved closer to rub her shoulder. "It's okay. We'll figure out a way to get him back for you."

"How did you know Kathy could help you?" Samantha asked.

Both Scarlett and Kathy looked at her, confused.

"If you knew that a witch locked Oliver away, what made you think that Kathy was someone who could help you free him?" Samantha didn't like the fact that this woman just showed up into their lives and wanted them to fix her problems for her.

"I recognized her aura when I saw her in the mall today," Scarlett said.

Kathy nodded. "I thought it was kooky at first, too, but I didn't tell her I was a witch and she just knew."

"Yeah, it's the fact that she just knew that's getting me."

"You don't believe her?" Kathy asked.

Scarlett held out her hand to stop Kathy, then turned to Samantha. "What if I prove that what I say is true?"

"How?" Samantha asked.

"I see that you're married." Scarlett indicated the wedding ring on Samantha's finger. "If you'd like, I can help you relive the moment you first met the love of your life."

"You can do that?" Kathy asked with the hint of a smile. Scarlett nodded. "It would require me to perform magic on you."

Samantha waved her hands and shook her head. "Nope. No way. I'm not going to allow you to cast a spell on me to get you to trust me."

"Sam, what do you think is going to happen?" Kathy asked.

"It's a memory she's bringing to the surface. Besides, I'm here. Steven's here."

"If I end up braindead, what good is it going to do if you two are here?" Samantha asked.

"Okay, but wouldn't your mind specialty help you protect yourself against any funny business like that?" Kathy asked.

Samantha considered this, as well as the idea that she could use her specialty to probe Scarlett's mind. But she wasn't getting a good read on the enchantress, which concerned her. However, she was also not on her A-game, so the lack of vibes coming from Scarlett could've been Samantha's own issue.

Sighing, Samantha said, "Fine. Let's make it quick. I already have a headache."

"This won't hurt at all. You'll just feel like you're going to sleep." Scarlett stepped forward.

"As if I haven't slept enough today." Samantha adjusted herself on the couch. "Okay. I'm ready."

With two fingers, Scarlett touched Samantha's forehead and in an instant, the whole world slipped away.

CHAPTER 20

- FEBRUARY 1985 -

Samantha's back ached as she hunched over her textbook in the library. It was only three weeks into her second semester of college and she was already stressed out to the max. Was this how the next three years were going to go?

She rubbed her eyes and scanned the table for the one sheet of paper on tax law that she had been reviewing when she first sat down. That was likely four hours ago. Definitely before the sun had set.

The one plus side of coming to the library so late was that there weren't very many people here. She could commandeer a whole table to help her spread out her thoughts.

The downside to coming to the library so late was that she had skipped dinner. Again. It was essentially her only option because they were short on cash, like they always were. Kathy was already working two jobs and Samantha spent the day going to her morning classes, working an eight-hour shift through the afternoon, only to return to the library for several hours to finish up her homework before she had to do it all over again the next day.

It was an insane routine—and not a healthy one—but it was the only way she could hold it all together.

Trying to focus on her textbook again, Samantha mindlessly pulled her hair up on top of her head to get it out of her face. She felt a few strands touch her forehead and she brushed them away. She knew she probably didn't look that great, but she didn't care about appearances. She cared about passing her Tax Law class.

"You look like you're struggling."

Samantha's head snapped up to the guy sitting two tables away from her. It was the first time she had looked up since she sat down and she realized they were the only two in there, besides the librarian working at the reference desk behind them.

She rubbed her forehead. "Um…yeah, a little."

"If it's math, I work with the tutoring center doing that," he said. "I could help if you need it."

Samantha gave him a tight smile. "Thanks, but I think I'll be okay."

"Okay," he said with a nod. "Good luck."

Turning back to her textbook, she read the next paragraph.

Then reread it, before focusing in on the sentence that was catching her up. What did 'legal reserve' mean again?

She reached for another sheet of paper from the table, looked up the definition, then turned back to her textbook to reread the paragraph a third time. Finally, it made sense.

Turning to her homework, she read the first problem and her mind spun. She couldn't figure out exactly what they were asking. Skipping it, she moved on to the next, which offered a scenario and asked for the dollar amount the person would pay in their taxes.

Pulling out her calculator, she figured the number and wrote it down. Then stared at it. How was it possible they were supposed to pay *more* in taxes than their annual gross income? It didn't make sense.

She sighed heavily, then looked up at the guy across the room. He was stuffing his books in his backpack.

"Oh, are you leaving?" she asked.

"I'm beat," he said. "How much longer are you staying? Do you want me to walk you out?"

"Actually…" She looked down at the mess she had created on the table. "I was hoping your offer for help still stood."

Smiling, he zipped up his bag and stepped over to her table. "What are you working on?"

"Well, it's not exactly math," she said. "More like…math adjacent."

He laughed. "Well, my major is accounting, so it's probably

a safe bet that I can help. Oh, Tax Law, I took this last year. Talk about a brutal class."

"Tell me about it." She pulled out the chair beside her. "Here, have a seat. I'm so confused."

He lowered himself in the seat beside her. "This is my second year and I'll tell you that everything makes more sense after enduring the harshness of Tax Law last year."

"Silver lining, I suppose." She indicated the second problem. "I definitely messed this one up."

He nodded. "Yup, I'd say you did."

"So can you help?"

"I don't know. My rates have increased from the first offer."

Samantha hooked an eyebrow. He was cute, but she wasn't in the mood to play games. "Never mind, I'll figure it out."

"It was a joke," he said.

Sighing again, she swiped at the pesky strand of hair that kept brushing against her forehead. "I know. I'm just so stressed out."

"Well, first of all, relax. It's not going to get any easier if you work yourself up. Second, let's think this through."

He pulled her textbook over to him and scanned it. As he read through the book, he offered explanations in layman's terms so Samantha could understand the concepts. After working through the chapter, they tackled the review questions together and she figured out what exactly she did wrong on the second problem.

"The homework was harder than the exams with this class," he said. "And the beginning of the semester was definitely harder than the second half, but that's because we built on what we learned at the beginning."

Samantha breathed out a sigh of relief now that her homework was done for the day. She collected her papers. "Thanks so much for your help. That probably would've taken me another hour or two on my own."

"No problem. If you need any help again, just let me know." He offered his hand. "I'm Steven Harper."

She shook it. "Samantha Walker."

"Nice to meet you."

Her eyes drifted to the clock on the wall. "Shoot, is it nine o'clock already? I need to catch the bus! It's the last one of the night!"

As she stuffed her papers into her own backpack, Steven said, "I could drive you home if you want."

Rising to her feet, she hauled the overstuffed bag onto her aching back. "I appreciate that, but getting in a car at night with a man I just met does not sound promising. As much as I appreciate the offer—and your help with my homework—I'm going to have to pass."

She led him out onto 7th Street, where they proceeded to her bus stop on Peach Street. The breeze was cold and the snow crunched under their feet, but Samantha's belly burned with nerves as she talked to Steven.

"So this is your first year?" he asked.

"Is it that obvious?"

He held up his hands. "Hey, no judgment here. We all need to start somewhere. This is my second year."

"Yeah, you mentioned that. And you're in the accounting program?"

He nodded. "You too?"

"Yeah. Where are you planning on working after graduation? Personal taxes?"

Steven groaned. "Eh, maybe. I'm thinking more corporate accounts, quarterly taxes. That type of thing."

She nodded. "That'd be interesting."

"Is that what you're thinking about too?"

"I don't really know yet," she admitted. "Personal finance makes sense to me, but that's because it's what I've been exposed to most, dealing with my own bills and everything. But I like the idea of working with numbers that won't make or break someone's livelihood."

"In our profession, people try to avoid us at all costs until they need us."

She smiled. "Very true."

They crossed Peach Street and Samantha could already see the bus coming, which she was a little disappointed to see.

"This is my stop," she said. "Thanks for everything."

"Do you want to study again sometime?" he offered.

"I'd like that," she said, then added, "I also like to go out to eat sometimes." Cringing, she added, "I meant, if you'd like to take me."

To her relief, Steven laughed. "That sounds better than studying. And it sounds like a date. Are you in the book? I'll call you."

She smiled and readjusted her backpack strap. "I'd like that."

CHAPTER 21

When Samantha woke up from Scarlett's spell, she had a smile on her face. To her surprise, her headache had faded as well. The memory of meeting Steven for the first time put her in a state of bliss, where all of her other ailments faded.

"Did it work?" Kathy asked from beside her.

"It did." Samantha turned to Scarlett. "How did you do that? It was so vivid. As if I were reliving it all over again. I wasn't just seeing it, I was feeling it." Again, her lips curled into a smile. The nerves she felt that night had erupted in her belly again, especially as she thought of how far they'd come in the last four years.

Scarlett grinned. "That's my specialty."

"You have a mind specialty too?" Kathy asked.

"No. I have a love specialty."

"Well, now that you've proven that you are who you say you are," Samantha said, "how do we find Ella? If she's on tour, she could be in any city."

"I could call the Warner and see if someone could get ahold of the tour schedule," Kathy suggested.

"There's no need for that," Scarlett said. "I've tracked them down. They'll be back in Buffalo by Saturday."

"Buffalo? But you said they were there last year," Kathy said. "Don't they normally travel to different places? Buffalo doesn't seem like a huge market."

Samantha gave her sister a look. "Since when did you become an expert on tour markets?"

Kathy shrugged. "I'm just saying…"

"They are on the tail-end of the tour," Scarlett clarified. "They're only staying in Buffalo after several shows in Toronto. Moving that many people across the border with all of that equipment and props and staging takes time. They're not going to be in Buffalo for long. I would imagine they'd continue on to New York on Sunday."

Sunday. As in only three days away. Which meant that if they were going to help Scarlett and stop Ella, they had a deadline.

"How did you track them down?" Samantha asked. "A tour schedule wouldn't show what cities they were stopping in just to rest."

"True, but I keep in touch with a couple of the girls I used to work with," Scarlett said. "They haven't seen Oliver, but they say Ella is still in the cast."

"Don't they wonder why you're asking about them?" Kathy asked.

"They were there when Oliver and I fell in love," Scarlett said. "They know our story—at least, part of it. They just think I quit the show to run away with Oliver after Ella and I fought over him."

"How do you know he's not just back at his apartment in Buffalo? Away from both you and Ella?" Samantha asked.

Kathy swatted at her sister for the insensitive comment.

"What?" Samantha rubbed her arm and glared at her sister. "I'm just saying, it's a possibility."

"He would've reached out to me," Scarlett said. "I know he would've. He was the one who first pursued me. He's the one who wanted me to stay in Buffalo with him. He's the one who had more faith in our relationship than I did." She wiped away tears from her eyes.

"And now you're the one who is going to save your love," Kathy offered. "And we'll help."

"Kathy," Samantha said as a warning.

"What?"

The older sister shook her head. "I'm still not convinced."

"You, of all people, should be able to sense the sincerity in

Scarlett," Kathy said. "She's speaking from her heart—and it's breaking. If we can help with that, why wouldn't we?" With her sister's continued pause, Kathy added, "She used her power on you, now use your power on her."

Samantha leaned forward and looked into Scarlett's eyes. She focused all her energy on trying to scope out ill-intentions coming from Scarlett's direction but couldn't sense any.

"Well?" Kathy asked.

Samantha straightened up and kept her eyes on Scarlett. "So you know that Ella is in Buffalo, but where specifically? Do you have a way of tracking her once we get there?"

Scarlett dropped her head. "I was hoping that was something the two of you could help me with."

Samantha gave her sister a look, who seemed perfectly okay with Scarlett's statement. Samantha, on the other hand, wanted to be sure they weren't being taken advantage of. Or walking into a trap.

"My powers—and, honestly, most of my intentions—are motivated by love," Scarlett said. "As an enchantress, I'm limited in my abilities, except when it comes to love. And whatever Ella's done has cloaked Oliver and prevented me from connecting with his heart. I need your help in finding him."

"Sam, put yourself in her shoes," Kathy said. "Remember when Steven was taken by the shapeshifter and your telepathic power didn't work in that house party? You needed to rely on me to help, right?"

"That's different," she said. "You're my sister."

"So what? You still couldn't do it on your own. Scarlett needs our help."

Samantha knew that was true. Scarlett had every reason to ask for help, but reconnecting two people in love was the work of an *enchantress*, not a witch. Witches saved and protected people from evil.

"It's not in my instinctive nature to fight," Scarlett said. "And I fear with Ella's power, it may come down to a fight. She has abilities that I cannot compete with."

Ignoring her sister, Kathy turned to Scarlett and said, "We'll be able to track down Oliver, no problem. We just need something of his to tie to the ritual to make it stronger."

"Like what?"

"A piece of jewelry that he always wore, clothing, even a note that he left might work," Kathy explained. "The more personal the item, the better."

Scarlett nodded. "I think I have something in mind."

They both turned to Samantha, waiting to see if she would finally agree to help, but the older witch sat in silence.

Everyone's attention turned toward the back of the house, where Steven emerged from the kitchen with a dish towel over his shoulder. "Dinner's ready, for whoever's hungry."

The three women stared at him. The reality of having dinner, as well as household chores, was a complete contrast to the conversation they had been having.

ENCHANTRESS

"Is everything okay?" he asked.

Samantha turned to her husband. "Kathy and I need to go to Buffalo."

CHAPTER 22

"Are you mad at me?" Jeremy asked as he followed Kathy down the hallway at Porreco College. "I called you the last two nights and got no response!"

"You think there might be a reason for that?"

She was annoyed to see him waiting for her when she got out of class. All night long, she thought of Jeremy and Lisa, and how Kathy was the one who needed to bow out.

Eventually, her thoughts turned to the only one who knew the whole story: Jeremy. He was the one who should've been honest from the beginning. He was the one who was essentially getting the best of both worlds by seeing both women. Even though Kathy knew it probably wasn't an intentional act, it still annoyed her.

"I would assume there is a reason, but I don't know what it is." He followed her to the foyer, where he caught her arm and made her look at him. "Kathy, what's going on? Let's talk about it."

"I ran into Lisa yesterday at the store," she said.

His face dropped. "Oh."

"Yeah. And she told me that the two of you have been seeing each other for a while."

"Kathy, it's not like that—"

"So she's lying? You haven't been seeing her?"

"No, that's not it. I—"

"Then you were lying to me," she said. "Because you made it sound like you were single and had no problems with getting back together with me."

He sighed. "Okay, yes. Lisa and I have been dating casually for a bit now."

Kathy turned toward the door, but he reached for her again.

"But it's not serious," he said. "And we've made no commitments to each other. You and I were long broken up before I started seeing Lisa. And I didn't expect for you and I to…you know, at your sister's wedding. I was genuinely there to be supportive of them."

She could feel her anger slip away, but still she said, "If you were seeing Lisa—even casually—then you never should've slept with me that night. And you should've been honest about it. *You* were the one who kissed *me* that night."

"I know, but Kathy, I can't help it that there's a spark between us," he said. "I didn't realize quite how strong it was until I saw you again and—I couldn't help myself."

She rolled her eyes for show, but she agreed with him. There was something between them that seemed to draw them together. Even now, while she was annoyed with him, she still wanted him to reach for her hand and take her for a drive somewhere so they could forget any of this ever happened.

But that wasn't reality.

"I should've been honest from the beginning," he said. "I'm sorry. After we reconnected, I just didn't know how to bring it up without an argument."

Kathy sighed. "I can see that. But I don't like being played like that and I certainly don't like being lied to."

"I didn't lie. I just didn't tell the whole truth."

She shot him a look.

"Okay, you're right," he said. "It's the same thing. And again, I'm sorry. Let me make it up to you. What are you doing tonight?"

"Packing."

That threw him off. "Packing? For what?"

"I'm going out of town this weekend with Samantha."

"Where?"

Kathy instantly regretted blurting out what she was going to be doing because it would generate a list of questions that she couldn't exactly answer. *Saving a man from the grasps of an evil witch in order to reunite him with his enchantress lover* just didn't roll off the tongue easily. "We're going to Buffalo," she finally said.

"What are you doing up there?"

"Um…helping a friend."

"Are they moving or something? I could help."

She turned and tried to brush him off, but he followed. "I don't really know the situation. Samantha set it up."

Jeremy jogged to catch her before she exited. "Let me drive you up there. We could talk on the way, figure out a plan forward for us."

"No, Jeremy, I don't know how long we're going to be gone or—" *Or if anything bad is going to happen*, she finished in her head. Instead, she remained vague. "Or anything like that."

"Have you or Samantha ever been to Buffalo?"

"Once, a long time ago with our dad."

"And it's just the two of you?"

"Yes, it is." Her response was short, already tired of the questions. "What's your point?"

"I used to go to Buffalo every summer when I was growing up," he said. "I would stay for a couple weeks with my cousin and his family. I could help you navigate the city."

Kathy considered it. Neither she nor Samantha knew their way around Buffalo and Scarlett was from out near New York City. If Oliver was hiding out somewhere, it'd save them time to not have to figure out the layout of the city.

But what excuse would she give Jeremy for running around with a woman she had just met in search of a man they'd never met? Would a simple memory-altering spell after the trip be enough to erase it from his mind? Would Samantha's mind specialty be able to pinpoint which parts to let Jeremy forget and which to allow him to keep? If they really did get a chance to talk about their relationship, Kathy wanted him to remember that.

"You really want to come, don't you?" she asked.

He nodded and took her hands in his. "I want to apologize for the whole misunderstanding. If you want, I'll break up with Lisa tonight after work." He checked his watch. "Which I should be getting back to. My lunch break is almost over."

Kathy shook her head. "I don't want you to break up with Lisa just to get back together with me. That's not fair."

"Even if I still love you?"

She studied him. Last summer, the siren's magic proved they weren't actually in love, but Scarlett had told her that a man who was once in love actually meant it. Maybe there was something to the saying: absence makes the heart grow fonder.

"Easy there," she said with a smirk. "Let's wait to unpack all of *that* until we have a chance to talk."

He laughed. "So you're going to let me come with you?"

She looked into his eyes and saw the happiness. The fact that he wanted to just spend time with her was one of the things she wished were different back when they broke up. Kathy knew that she'd changed. Maybe Jeremy had too. Maybe their relationship would work out this time around.

"We're leaving at six o'clock tonight, not a minute later," she said. "When we get to the hotel, you're going to need to get your own room."

He smiled. "I won't be late."

CHAPTER 23

Are you feeling any better?"

Samantha kept her hands busy as she packed up the small suitcase open on her bed. She tried not to let her husband's concerns annoy her, but she was tired of him asking if she was okay. And it had only been two days since she had started to feel sick.

"I don't like the idea of you going away this weekend if you're not feeling well," he added.

"I feel fine." She slipped a few vials of a power-stripping potion into the side pocket of her suitcase. They were still warm from being recently brewed. She had come home early to work on them in case that was the only way they could stop Ella. Neither her nor Kathy had any idea what they were up against with this witch. And Scarlett offered no further insight.

Whether that was intentional or innocent, Samantha wasn't sure. She tried not to dwell on it.

"But you're not fine," he said. "Samantha, yesterday you passed out at work and spent the rest of the day sleeping!"

She busied herself by folding the pile of clothes she had pulled out of the dryer on her way upstairs. "And today I feel fine."

He crossed his arms and stared at her across the bed. "Are you being honest with me?"

For the first time, her eyes met his. "Are you saying you think I'm lying?"

"You have a habit of self-sacrificing for other people." He shrugged. "So yeah, maybe you are lying."

Turning her attention back to the few remaining clothes to fold, she murmured, "I'm going."

"And I don't think you should. Even if you felt fine today, the extra sleep and rest this weekend will help you recover to one hundred percent."

There was no arguing there. He had a point. This was not what she thought she'd be doing on her Friday evening after a long week. And as she heard the wind whip around the trees outside, she dreaded going back out into the cold.

But she'd made a promise to Scarlett, who had been waiting downstairs all day, very patient for the witches' help, despite the ticking deadline. Samantha was not about to let her down.

"Steven, your concern is noted." She zipped up her suitcase and leaned forward on it toward him. "And I love you for it, but trust me, I know my own body. I'm fine."

Even she wasn't believing her own lie. Truth be told, she felt like *something* was off about her all day. She just couldn't put her finger on it. And until she had a definitive problem with a definitive solution, she had a life to live and people to save.

"Besides," she added, "my job as a witch is calling me away, regardless of how I feel. I'm not going to send Kathy up to Buffalo alone, especially since we don't know what we're up against. With the two of us together, we'll put that evil witch in her place and be back by Sunday. Plenty of time before Tuesday."

His brow scrunched in exaggerated confusion. "You think I want you to stay because of *Valentine's Day*?"

It was their first as a married couple.

Samantha set her suitcase on the floor by the door and turned to straighten the blankets on the bed. "Way to sweep me off my feet with a V-Day surprise, honey."

He came around the bed and took her hands. "Samantha, I'm worried about your wellbeing. I want to spend *every* Valentine's Day with you for the rest of my life, but that's not going to happen if you start being reckless."

She pulled her hands away from his and placed them on either side of his face. "Steven, if you think this weekend is the start of me being a bit reckless, then you married the wrong girl. You knew what you were getting into when you said, 'I do.'

That's why I told you who I was *before* we got married." She kissed him quickly, hoping that would put an end to the conversation.

Steven followed her into the hall as she rolled her suitcase to the top of the stairs, ready to descend. "Well, if I can't change your mind about going, then I'm coming with you."

She studied him, trying to determine if he was bluffing. Why would he want to spend a weekend in Buffalo with only snippets of time spent with her, which would also include the presence of Kathy? Then again, what else would he do at home while she was nearly a hundred miles north?

And what would Kathy think? Would she be annoyed that their witch outing changed from a girl's trip to Steven tagging along? He'd be a fourth person and they might have to get a second hotel room, just for the sake of sanity. Not that that was an issue, now that money wasn't too much of a concern in their household.

"Are you serious?" she asked him to stall for time.

He nodded. "Dead serious, Sam. I'm not a fan of you chasing after all these weird things when you're feeling like yourself, but knowing your sick is only going to make it worse."

"So you want to come with me to babysit me?"

"To take care of you if you start to feel off," he said. "Or to try to convince you to slow down if you're too stubborn to admit that you're feeling sick."

Stubborn.

Was that what she was being with this whole Buffalo trip? She liked to think she was determined, but if things were different—if *Kathy* was the one who wasn't feeling great—Samantha would want her to sit this one out too.

Besides, Steven had genuine concerns about her health. He was sacrificing his own weekend to make sure she was okay. If that wasn't love, then she didn't know what love was. And if she was lucky enough to have someone who loved her and worried about her, she couldn't dismiss that. Especially so early into their marriage.

Above all else, she knew deep down that Steven had a point. It would be better if someone was keeping an eye out for her. Especially when she became so involved in stopping Ella and getting Oliver back that she didn't take a moment to take care of herself. For better or worse, she needed him.

"Okay," she said. "You can come."

Instantly, his face broke into a smile. "I can?"

"Yes, but you better hurry. We're leaving when Kathy gets home, and that should be soon."

CHAPTER 24

"Steven! Kathy's home!" Samantha called through the house to her husband when her sister walked through the front door. "We're leaving soon!" She turned to greet Kathy and her jaw went slack when she saw Jeremy step in behind her. "And she brought a friend…"

Kathy gave Samantha a sheepish look and closed the door behind them. "Yeah, about that…"

"Hello." Scarlett came around the corner from the living room and waved at Jeremy.

He offered her a smile and reached out to shake her hand. "Hi, I'm Jeremy."

She nodded. "Ah, right. Kathy's…friend."

Kathy's heart beat in her chest as she witnessed the

exchange. She needed to distract from any questions. "Anyway," she said loudly, "I'm *almost* ready to go. There's just one small thing—"

Samantha eyed her suspiciously. "What is it?"

Steven came out of the kitchen and set two bottles of water on the table near where his overnight bag sat. "Are we all set?"

"Just about," Kathy said. "Why don't you and Jeremy catch up? Sam and I need to talk alone for just a sec." She reached for her sister's arm and led her back toward the kitchen, but stopped and turned. "Uh, Scarlett, why don't you join us?"

Without another word, Scarlett followed the sisters to the back of the house.

"What's going on?" Samantha asked when they were alone.

"Jeremy's coming with us," Kathy said, then added quickly, "I know what you're going to say. But he used to go to Buffalo all the time when he was younger. He can be our navigator, even if it's just to get us there. Plus, he wanted to spend the weekend with me to—uh…he wanted to spend it with me and I didn't want to flat-out tell him no."

Scarlett studied the younger witch. "This is very important to her."

Samantha rubbed her forehead and sighed. "Okay."

"Okay? That's it?"

"Well, I have a little change too," Samantha said. "Steven's coming."

"So both of them are coming?" Kathy made a face. How

were they going to get anything done while keeping track of the guys? Then again, Steven could help with distracting Jeremy.

"Guess so," Samantha said. "I tried to talk him out of it, but he's worried because I haven't been feeling well."

Kathy's thoughts changed in an instant. "Are you sick?"

"I had a little mishap at work yesterday. It's no big deal, but it's got Steven all panicky."

"Are you sure you're okay?"

Samantha rolled her eyes. "Don't you start with that too."

Kathy put up her hands. "Okay! I won't push it. But promise me you'll be honest with yourself."

"Between you and Steven, there's no way I'd be able to lie if I wasn't feeling good." Seeing Kathy's look, she added, "I promise."

"Good. So it looks like this has turned out to be a group outing."

"Hopefully that doesn't come back to bite us in the ass."

"Yeah." Kathy turned to Scarlett. "Okay, before we get going, there's something you need to know: Jeremy doesn't know anything about magic. Doesn't know we're witches, doesn't know they exist, and certainly doesn't know about enchantresses."

"Is concealing pieces of your life something that will lead to a successful relationship?" Scarlett asked. "I'm just posing the question, I'm not trying to push you to one answer or another."

Kathy let out a heavy breath. "We're not at that level of trust yet. One step at a time. Either way, I'd like to keep the secret. We'll have to work on clever ways to keep it from him this weekend, but please don't say anything about magic or the real reason for our trip. He thinks we're helping you out, but doesn't know the specifics of it."

Scarlett nodded. "Keep quiet about magic around the guys. Got it."

"No, just Jeremy," Samantha said. "Steven knows everything—even though he sometimes doesn't *want* to know. So maybe you should keep quiet around him too, but if you slip around him it's not the end of the world."

The enchantress looked between the sisters, looking a little confused. "I'm very grateful of you helping me and Oliver, so please don't take this with any disrespect, but you two live very complicated love lives."

"It's not complicated." Kathy looked to her sister in effort to find the right words to describe their situations that didn't sound so bad. "Just the magic stuff is."

"Again, the only thing I will say of the matter is to pose the question: is hiding a large part of your life something you think will lead to a good relationship?"

The sisters were quiet as they really considered it. Finally, Samantha said, "I told Steven before we got married and I think it's helped us. He doesn't *like* the fact that I'm risking my life occasionally, but he understands it."

"You don't need to justify your relationship to me," Scarlett said. "As long as you and your partner are happy and content, that's all that matters. I just encourage you to be aware of seeds that seem to be innocent now that may be planted and may one day grow into uncontrollable weeds later."

"Well, thanks for the warning," Kathy said to change the subject. "Anyway, I'm all packed. We stopped at Jeremy's apartment on the way here and he packed his bag, so we're all ready to go if you are."

Jeremy's apartment was the same one in Lawrence Park that it had been before, with the same roommate, Michael. It was good to know that not everything had changed.

"Okay, if we're ready, then let's go." Samantha motioned for them to rejoin the guys in the foyer. "Our drive up there is about to be real cozy."

CHAPTER 25

"Are you sure Steven's not mad at me for making him share a room with Jeremy?" Kathy leaned forward on her bed in the hotel room. Her bag sat beside her and she debated whether she wanted to change before dinner.

Samantha paused before responding. "Well, I'm sure he's not *thrilled* with the idea. And I bet you're not going to be his favorite person for a while, but he understands."

"I'll have to make it up to him when we get back."

When they got to the hotel, they booked two rooms across the hall from each other. The girls took one while the guys took the other, per Kathy's request. Even though she and Jeremy had already hooked up once since they had reunited, she didn't want to blur anymore lines between them until they figured things out.

Especially if he was seeing Lisa. It was bad enough they were going away for the weekend together without Lisa knowing—albeit not *alone* together. That fact made Kathy feel dirty. Like she was sneaking around with a married man. Some people would find that exciting. She found it off-putting.

The separate rooms worked out well anyway because it allowed the witches to talk to Scarlett and develop a game plan without the interference of the guys and speaking in code because of Jeremy.

"We need to figure out what exactly we're doing," Samantha said from the second bed in the room. "We potentially only have a small window tomorrow to pull this off. It would help if we knew where to start."

Kathy turned to Scarlett, who was on the roll-away cot. "Do you know where we should start looking for Oliver?"

"We could try his apartment," Scarlett offered.

"But if he's been gone a year, chances are it's been cleaned out and rented to someone else," Samantha said. "I doubt he'd be there, but we could check if our other options run dry."

"What else you got?" Kathy tried to remain optimistic, if for no one else but Scarlett. "What about the venue where you two met?"

"I could take you there." Scarlett nodded slowly, her eyes drifting to the thin brown carpet.

"You don't sound so sure," Samantha said.

"It's just that I worry that I won't be a welcome face there if the cast returns for any reason," Scarlett explained. "I left quite abruptly. The cast, and certainly the director, probably never wants to see me again. To be honest, the crew at the venue might even blame me for Oliver disappearing. I thought he had run away, so I left so quickly that I didn't know what they were saying about me and Oliver in our absence."

"We'll just have to be careful then." Kathy sat up and unzipped her bag.

"What are you doing?" Samantha asked.

Kathy pulled out a large ceramic bowl that they used for location rituals.

"You brought that with you!"

"What else was I supposed to use, Sam?" Kathy countered as she stepped into the bathroom to fill it with water. "A styrofoam cup for the coffee? How the hell would we be able to see anything in that!"

"You could've brought something other than the *antique heirloom* that's irreplaceable!"

Kathy stepped out of the bathroom and set the bowl in the middle of the floor, where she sat cross-legged. "Relax. I'll be careful with it. Now shush while I try the ritual." She closed her eyes and began reciting:

> *I call on the strength of my power,*
> *show Oliver's face in the water.*

She repeated the spell again and again, only opening her eyes a peek to see if anything was happening.

Nothing.

"The ritual actually calls for four yellow candles," Samantha told Scarlett.

"Well, I thought the hotel would frown on an open flame in the room." Kathy motioned to the ceiling. "Especially if it set the sprinklers off." "Here." Samantha took a seat on the floor across from her sister and sat in a similar position. "Let's try it again with both of us."

Kathy took her sister's hands, again closed her eyes, and recited:

I call on the strength of my power,
show Oliver's face in the water.

Their chanting was abruptly interrupted by a knock on the door.

"Hey! Are you girls ready for dinner?" Steven asked on the other side.

"I'm starving!" Jeremy added, then quieter, "And bored."

"Just a minute!" Kathy called.

"Uh, we'll come get you when we're ready!" Samantha said. "Give us, like, five more minutes."

Guess that answered Kathy's earlier question. She wouldn't have time to change for dinner.

"Why isn't it working?" Scarlett asked after they heard the door across the hall close.

"We don't have a strong enough connection." Kathy stood and carried the bowl back to the bathroom, where she dumped the water down the sink.

"Perhaps I could try it," Scarlett suggested.

Samantha shrugged. "You could, I suppose, but I'm not sure what kind of effect it would have since you're not a witch. It'd be like me or Kathy trying to cast a spell to make someone fall in love with us. It'd work, to a degree, but not how we'd anticipate it to."

"What about something of Oliver's?" Kathy returned to the room as she dried the bowl with a towel. "Did you bring anything that he carried around with him a lot? Or something that was important to him?"

Scarlett reached for her own bag and pulled out a pocket knife. "He always had this in his pocket. In case he ever needed it." She smiled, and Kathy could tell she was recalling a happy memory of him.

"That's good," Samantha said. "Hold on to that. It'll help us strengthen the spell."

"So will casting it in a place that he has a connection to," Kathy added. "Like the theater venue or, what's more unlikely, his undisturbed apartment."

Scarlett nodded and closed her hand around the knife.

Samantha rubbed her shoulder. "We'll find him. I promise."

CHAPTER 26

Kathy looked up and down Main Street to make sure traffic had stopped at the light before she followed the rest of the group through the crosswalk to continue down North Street. It was cold, and the wind whipped against their faces until they stepped under the cover of the buildings that blocked the wind coming from the lake.

"Hey," Jeremy called Kathy back quietly as Samantha, Steven, and Scarlett carried on in front of them. Unfazed by the wind, Samantha and Steven walked hand-in-hand as they chit-chatted with Scarlett.

"What?" Kathy hunched her shoulders, as if to burrow herself deeper in her coat.

"We haven't had a chance to talk yet," he said. "I thought

maybe now was the perfect time."

They were on their way back to the hotel from dinner. Jeremy had suggested the Anchor Bar because it was right down North Street from their hotel and it was a Buffalo staple. Kathy thought the wings were good, but she didn't think the spicy food had helped Samantha feel any better.

"Sorry this turned out to be a group thing," Kathy said. The two of them fell into a slower pace, continuously putting distance between them and the other three. "Originally, it was just supposed to be me, Samantha, and Scarlett, but that obviously changed."

"Sorry," he said.

"No, it's okay. I'm glad you came. Otherwise, we probably would've opted for the restaurant in the hotel for all of our meals."

"Hey, they have great burgers, but I don't know if you'd want that in the morning."

She smiled to try to relieve the tension that persisted between them. "No, I don't think so."

"So who's Scarlett anyway? I know you said she's a friend, but I was talking to Steven and I got the impression that he doesn't know anything about her either."

"He probably just meant that he stays away from the girl chats." Kathy didn't want Jeremy to keep feeding that suspicion of Scarlett. Certainly not while they were all spending so much time together this weekend. "It's nice that you and Steven have been chatting. I'm sure he misses having a guy around to talk to."

Jeremy chuckled. "I didn't think I'd be forced to live with him again—in closer quarters than we did last time."

She made a face. "Sorry. I just didn't want the two of us to—"

"I get it," he said. "I just think it's funny, that's all."

The last time Kathy and Samantha had forced them all to cohabitate, it had destroyed Kathy and Jeremy's relationship. It wasn't until now that she realized she was pushing their limits yet again.

"If he starts snoring, just smack him with a pillow. It's only two nights."

"And then what?"

She shrugged, grateful for the distraction of having to cross the next intersection at Delaware Avenue. Up ahead, she could see the rest of the group walking up to the lobby of the hotel. Samantha looked back at Kathy, and the younger sister offered a wave to tell her that everything was okay. With that acknowledgement, Samantha turned and disappeared inside.

The light changed, flashing the white pedestrian sign, and Jeremy and Kathy stepped in front of headlights to cross, both silent. When they were safely across, Jeremy reached for Kathy's arm to stop her before she stepped into the hotel.

"Kathy, I know I pushed into your weekend, but we need to talk about us." He pulled at her arms until she slipped her hands out of her pockets and rested them in his. "If we're going to give us another shot—if I'm going to break off what I have with Lisa—I need to know that you're putting in an honest effort. I don't want to go through all of this just to break up again."

She nodded. "You're right. And I'm sorry for this crappy situation that is this weekend, but it's really important that I help Scarlett. I need to focus on helping her this weekend. Not that you're not important, but I already promised her this weekend before I promised you anything."

"Right, but tonight you weren't helping Scarlett," Jeremy said. "It was me who asked you to walk back with me. And I know it probably wasn't even on your mind because you're used to being on your own, but if I can't even have the small pockets of your time, then maybe that's my answer."

"No, Jeremy." Kathy shook her head. "I wasn't thinking. I do want to give us a shot and I *do* think it's important that we talk, but I've..." She sighed. "I've got a lot on my mind. I promise, we'll definitely have everything straightened out with Scarlett so that you and I can maybe have another Valentine's Day together. We have to keep the streak alive, even if a breakup was thrown in there."

They'd spent the last few years together for Valentine's Day. All the arguments and fights and other spats seemed to fizzle away every February 14th. Kathy had assumed that that phase of her life was over, but fate apparently had a different idea.

"I will make time for you for sure on Sunday," she promised.

"If not sooner. This is important to me too."

Jeremy leaned forward and kissed her cheek, pulling away with a smile. "That's all I needed to hear."

CHAPTER 27

"Oh wow, even up here is gorgeous!" Kathy exclaimed when they climbed the steps to the second floor of the theater lobby, which led to the balcony seats. She craned her neck and looked up at the ceiling.

Samantha, meanwhile, wasted no time setting up the location ritual. It was mid-morning and her, Kathy, and Scarlett hadn't exactly gotten clearance to be in Shea's Performing Arts Center unsupervised. Certainly not to perform magic. They had snuck through a back service door and made their way through the auditorium and into the lobby. The whole experience felt *wrong* to Samantha and she was anxious to get out as quickly as they could.

"Do you have the knife?" she asked Scarlett.

ENCHANTRESS

The enchantress passed over Oliver's knife as Samantha pulled out the ceramic bowl that Kathy had brought from home. When they left the hotel, Samantha hesitated bringing it to the theater with them for fear that it would shatter somehow, but she knew this was the best option they had for a viewing puddle.

Pulling out a bottle of water she had bought from a vending machine in the hotel lobby, Samantha unscrewed the top and dumped the contents into the bowl. She looked up at her sister, who was still wandering around the second floor looking at the architecture.

"Kathy, do you mind? I would like to get out of here sooner than later!" Samantha pulled out four yellow candles that she had brought with her, but didn't light them. She had no idea what kind of fire alarm system they had in this big old place and she didn't want to accidentally set it off. Instead, she aligned the unlit candles in the direction of north, south, east, and west and hoped that would be enough to call on their energies.

The younger witch whipped around at the sound of her name and came to join the other two by the bowl.

"Hopefully we'll be able to find Oliver, track him down without too many hiccups, and get back to the guys before they completely hate us," Samantha said.

"Sorry," Scarlett murmured.

Kathy put her arm around their new friend. "Hey, we're all just trying to get back to the people in our lives, right? We're going to help you with that."

Earlier that morning, the five of them had all had breakfast together, which must've sent the message that the girls were free to spend the day with Steven and Jeremy. Much to their disappointment, Samantha suggested that Steven and Jeremy spend the day together while the girls helped Scarlett. Which meant that for the guys, every passing minute was being counted until the girls could return.

"All right," Samantha started, "Kathy and I are going to be the ones who actually cast the spell, but Scarlett, I think it'd help make it stronger if you were part of the circle holding Oliver's knife. You have the biggest connection to him, so having you in the circle will only strengthen our call to him."

Scarlett nodded. "So no chanting?"

"Not by you," Samantha said.

"Just hold our hands," Kathy added.

"Ready?"

Scarlett nodded nervously. "I think so."

"We'll find him," Kathy promised.

Samantha wasn't so sure. They had performed this location ritual plenty of times without any good results. Case in point: Kathy's attempt last night. Luckily, they had a few more tools this time to give it a bit more *oomph*.

The three of them joined hands, and Samantha and Kathy recited the spell together.

ENCHANTRESS

After the third chant, the reflection in the water began to form to show something other than the lights reflecting from the ceiling.

"I think I see him!" Scarlett exclaimed.

"Keep chanting," Samantha said, before reciting the spell again with her sister.

With each repetition, the reflection in the water became clearer, although it was still difficult to determine what exactly it showed. It was clearly a man they were looking at—Oliver, as Scarlett clarified—but his immediate surroundings looked like nothing Samantha had ever seen. Like a desert or a grave or something.

Beyond that, his outer surroundings weren't a box, like a grave would be. Instead, it looked almost transparent, even if a bit warped. And it wasn't dirt he was laying on, but sand.

"Is that an…*hourglass*?" Kathy asked.

"Isn't this trespassing?" a woman's voice said from behind them.

The three of them instantly withdrew their hands from one another and turned to face the woman who walked up the stairs.

"Ella, where did you put him?" Scarlett asked as she rose to her feet.

"Someplace you'll never find him."

Samantha stepped beside Scarlett, taking a step forward to put the enchantress just behind her. "Tell us before we're forced to do something that you'll—"

With the wave of her hand, Ella sent the ceramic bowl crashing against the wall, shattering it into pieces. Along with it, the image of wherever Oliver was being held captive.

CHAPTER 28

So much for that heirloom," Kathy muttered to herself. She put up her hands to freeze the evil witch, but Ella lifted her hand and Kathy felt herself suddenly soar through the air. She landed on her butt about ten feet back from where she had just been standing.

Scarlett rushed to Kathy's side, throwing a hateful look toward Ella once she reached her. "Leave them alone!"

Samantha stepped toward Ella, making intense eye-contact so that the evil witch couldn't turn away. "Tell me where you're keeping Oliver."

Kathy knew her sister was trying her persuasion power out. If Samantha had more time, she could probably also try picking through Ella's mind to find the information herself, but

Samantha wasn't as well-versed in that area of expertise yet and they certainly didn't have time to sit around and let her try it.

"Oliver," Ella muttered.

"Yes, where did you put him?" Samantha pushed. "You want to tell me. You're tired of hiding this secret from everyone."

"I have…I have him…I have him in…"

Something is wrong, Kathy thought.

Samantha was losing her pull on Ella, although Kathy didn't think it had anything to do with Ella's strength as a witch. Samantha looked a little more haggard than she usually did. Like the exertion of magic when they performed the location ritual had sucked a lot of power out of her.

Ella shook her head and returned to her senses. Kathy again lifted her hands to freeze, but all Ella needed to do was flick her fingers and Samantha tumbled backward toward Scarlett and Kathy.

"Stay here," Kathy instructed Scarlett. She turned back to the witch. "You're making enemies with the wrong people, lady!" She stepped forward as Ella sprinted toward her, meeting her before Kathy could use her power.

Grabbing ahold of Kathy's wrists, Ella brought her knee up to try to hit Kathy in the stomach, but she moved out of the way in time. The two struggled, and Kathy managed to grab ahold of Ella's arms with her hands, but Ella sent out a burst of invisible energy right at Kathy's chest that sent the witch flying back toward her sister.

Kathy groaned as she rolled on her back. This was the second time she had landed on her ass in a matter of minutes. Yet, she was more concerned about Samantha, who seemed out of it before she even took a flight down the hall.

"You okay, Sam?"

"Peachy." Samantha grimaced as she nursed her wrist, rolling her hand to loosen it.

Kathy helped her sister up. "We've gotta get that hourglass."

Ella reached for something in her coat pocket and pulled out a small hourglass that enlarged on her outstretched palm. "Is this what you're looking for?"

Kathy turned to Ella and took a step forward, but noticed Samantha out of the corner of her eye. She clung to the decorative chair rail along the wall, swaying on her feet.

"Sam, are you sure you're okay?"

In response, her older sister bent over and hurled all over the architecture that Kathy had just been admiring.

CHAPTER 29

Scarlett watched as Samantha vomited on the floor and Kathy rushed to her side. Her heart had been racing through the encounter, hoping that they could get the hourglass in hand. But it wasn't turning out in their favor. Now both witches were preoccupied and Ella was free to run away and escape.

She couldn't let that happen.

In a split-second decision, Scarlett chased after Ella down the staircase to the main lobby. It wasn't hard to follow her since the lobby was empty.

Ella pulled open the door beneath the main stairs and disappeared within.

When Scarlett whipped open the door to enter herself, she

paused for only a fraction of a second as she was hit with startling dark, dankness compared to the opulent room of the lobby. Even when she had been part of the crew last year, she hadn't really ever ventured into the lobby or the various doorways off of it. Still, she quickly regained her composure and descended the wooden stairs into what she assumed was the basement.

Down in the cellar, Scarlett's attention was momentarily captivated by the various discarded set pieces, props, and racks of wardrobe clothing that were stashed in makeshift rooms divided only by chain-link fencing. A way to section off what pieces fit with each stage production, according to the sign hooked to the gate door of each room.

With just a quick glance, Scarlett could see that Ella was not in any of the storage rooms in the vicinity, which meant she needed to venture deeper into the labyrinth of basement cage rooms. The whole place was dimly lit and particularly chilly, although it wasn't damp. That would ruin the errant props that were stored down here, so Scarlett was sure any moisture issues that arose were immediately taken care of.

From around the corner, one of the cage doors clanged. Scarlett ignored her irrational fears of the dark and jogged to meet the sound and catch up to Ella.

When Scarlett came around, she saw one of the cage doors was swinging on its hinges. The interior beyond the chain-link fence wall was shrouded by multiple racks of clothing. Worse, it was dark because the nearby light had been shattered.

"Ella, you're only trapping yourself down here." Scarlett slowly stepped into the room and peered around. "If we talk about this, maybe we can—"

The door behind her slammed shut, telling Scarlett that she had ventured too far away from the entrance. She knew she should've left herself an escape route but now it was too late.

Ella appeared on the other side, pulling a set piece over in front of the door—a large dining room table that had nicks and scratches and cobwebs all over it.

The enchantress banged on the fencing. "Let me out!" She thought that maybe with enough force that she could push the table out of the way to wiggle out of the room. But it was no use. The table was solid and it wasn't going anywhere.

"I believe *you're* the one who walked into a trap," Ella said with a chuckle. "I'm surprised you came back at all."

"I found some people who could help me get Oliver away from you." Scarlett tried pulling the door inward, but the hinges wouldn't allow it. She debated whether she could break them off, but knew it would take some work. If she tried too hard to free herself in front of Ella, she might only be subjecting herself to a spell.

"When you quit the show and left town, you gave up any right you have to Oliver."

"Don't you think we should let Oliver decide?" Scarlett asked. "Without the influence of magic?"

"Says the woman who is losing."

"So then ask yourself this: is it really love if you need to keep him captive?"

Ella's eyes grew large in rage. "Why don't you focus on a new love? I would think the witches you partnered with both have eligible men. Try this!" Turning her nose up, Ella recited:

Divert your eyes to someone new,
One of the witches' men will do!

A light appeared over Scarlett, illuminating the caged room, but faded quickly. Scarlett took a quick mental assessment but didn't determine any difference in the way she was acting or thinking. Yet she wasn't ready to celebrate the failure of Ella's spell yet. The witch's powers had certainly grown in the last year—she'd proved that upstairs—so maybe her spellcasting had too.

"That'll keep you preoccupied for a while," Ella said. "By time your new friends figure out what happened to you, Oliver and I will be long gone!" She turned and hurried down the makeshift corridor, deeper into the darkness.

"Ella! Come back and reverse this spell!" Scarlett yelled after her. "You can't just leave me here!"

"Scarlett?" Kathy's voice called from the direction of the lobby.

"I'm over here!"

Kathy and her sister emerged from the shadows.

"Oh my gosh, what happened?" Kathy pushed against the old dining room table to move it out of the way.

"Ella trapped me in here." Scarlett pushed open the gate and stepped out to join the sisters. "Thanks for helping me. I'm sorry I went and screwed everything up."

Samantha shook her head. "You didn't screw anything up."

"I think I might've, though," Scarlett said. "Ella cast a spell on me."

The sisters exchanged glances. Although Scarlett wasn't a witch, she knew that that look wasn't good. And neither was their chances of saving Oliver.

CHAPTER 30

O kay, we'll just go back to the room quick to regroup." Kathy fumbled with the key as she walked down the hallway. "Talk about our options and then go find Ella and get Oliv—"

"There you guys are!" Jeremy called out from behind them down the hallway.

The girls all turned just outside their hotel rooms as the guys joined them. Jeremy had a plastic bag with what looked like subs.

"Lunch?" Kathy asked.

"Joe's Deli!" he said with a big smile that only drew blank stares from the rest of them.

"He's been raving about this place since I suggested we get

something to eat," Steven muttered from behind him.

"It's this little place on Hertel," Jeremy said. "Fantastic food, local, old-school. I love it!"

"It smells good," Samantha said.

"Yeah," Kathy agreed. "So your guy-date went well?"

The smile faded quickly from Jeremy's face and Steven looked away. Both grumbled something to the effect of, "It was all right."

"So if you're back, does that mean you guys are done then?" Jeremy asked.

"Not quite," Kathy said.

"Sam, are you okay?" Steven asked. "You don't look so good."

Kathy glanced over at her sister and saw the same squeamish face she had earlier. She also thought that the smell of the subs—which was quickly filling up the crowded hallway—might've been what was setting her sister's stomach off.

"I'm fine," Samantha told him.

"Sam…" he pushed.

Sensing an argument brewing, Kathy put up a hand toward Steven's chest. "I've been keeping an eye on her. It's okay." She turned to Jeremy. "What kind of subs did you get?"

"Jimmy's Cuban! Ham, swiss, pickles, honey mustard." Jeremy moaned. "And Steven got something boring, like a turkey club or something."

Steven ignored the jab, too focused on his wife.

"Scarlett, would you mind keeping the guys company?" Kathy asked before Steven could pull Samantha away. Based on his reaction—and what happened in the lobby at Shea's—she knew she was missing something and needed an explanation. "I would like to have a quick chat with my sister."

Brightening up, Scarlett said, "Of course!"

"It'll just be a minute," Kathy promised.

Jeremy pulled the keys from his pocket and opened the door for Scarlett. Steven, however, lingered in the hallway. He was trying to make eye contact with Samantha, who was desperately avoiding it.

Kathy slid the key in her own lock and opened the door. Grabbing ahold of Samantha's arm, she nearly dragged her sister inside. "It'll be fine, Steven. I've got her."

Reluctantly, he turned toward his room, but propped the door open. Kathy made sure he disappeared around the corner before closing hers.

Something was going on and she didn't like not knowing what it was.

CHAPTER 31

W e're a team, right?" Kathy asked Samantha when they were alone.

Samantha felt like a child, being pushed around by her younger sister, but she gave in because it was easier than arguing. She sat on the end of her bed, feeling as though her body was drained of all of its energy. The fight with Ella had suddenly exhausted her. "Of course we are."

"Then why don't you tell me what the *hell* is going on?" Kathy stood with her hands on her hips and stern look on her face.

Samantha wrapped her arms around herself and shrugged. "I don't really know." No point in lying. Between Steven and Kathy, apparently she was more transparent than she had thought she was.

"Are you sick?"

"Maybe."

"You look it."

Samantha shot Kathy a look. "Thanks."

"I'm serious, Sam. You've never thrown up during a fight before. Is this why Steven is being such a helicopter?"

"A helicopter?"

"He's hovering over you like a puppy with separation anxiety! What's the deal? I know he wouldn't voluntarily come on a magical outing unless something was up, and based on today, something *is* up. Spill."

Samantha sighed. How much was she going to reveal to be honest with her sister but not create another panicked monster that would *helicopter* over her like Steven was?

Still, she knew that the two people closest to her would find out eventually. Better to be honest and upfront about it and kill any dangerous wonderings that might be going on in Kathy's head.

"I've been feeling off lately," she started. "Ever since Wednesday when Steven and I went to look at that townhouse."

"Off how?"

"Sick to my stomach, sensitive to smells, tired."

Kathy nodded, but didn't offer anything further.

"And then on Thursday I…passed out at work."

"You *passed out*?" Kathy echoed. "Why didn't you tell me?"

"Because I was embarrassed by it! And I went home, spent the rest of the day in bed. Besides, you were gone all day."

"And then I came home with Scarlett and unloaded all of this on you." Kathy sighed and took a seat on the other bed. "What else is there?"

"Nothing. Yesterday I felt fine all day at work. This morning I woke up feeling good. Then I got tossed around a bit by Ella and next thing I know I'm throwing up."

"Are you pregnant?"

Samantha didn't say anything for a long time. And Kathy didn't push the issue, allowing her sister time to respond when she was ready to.

"I thought of that," she finally said. "So on my way home on Thursday, I bought a test and I took it while everyone was gone."

"And?"

"It was negative."

"But all of the signs—"

"I know," Samantha said. "But I took another one yesterday on my lunch break. Another negative. And yet I still feel off. I'm not myself, Kathy." She could feel her voice start to shake as she lost control. "What if this is something bad?"

Kathy rose and came to sit beside her sister, wrapping her arm around her. "Whatever it is, we'll figure it out and it'll be okay. You're not alone. You have me and now you have Steven. We're here for you."

Samantha leaned her head on her sister's shoulder and

wiped away tears from her cheeks. "Steven and I just got married and now I'm bringing this to him. I don't want to make him a widower."

"You're not going to make him a widower," Kathy said. "We'll figure it out."

The statement hung in the air. Something that neither witch really believed. They faced the unknown all the time, but this was perhaps the scariest thing that Samantha had ever faced. What if something really was wrong with her?

"What does Steven think about this?" Kathy asked.

"I haven't told him anything."

"Which is why he's been bugging you since we left."

"Right. I just don't know what to tell him because I don't know what's going on."

"Maybe you should see a doctor."

"And what if the issue is magical?"

"So then see a *witch* doctor."

"Are there really any that we can trust?" Samantha asked. "Didn't that shapeshifter from last fall say he got his abilities from a witch doctor claiming to be giving him treatments?"

"He never said she was a witch doctor."

"A witch who provides medical assistance through magical remedies is a witch doctor."

Kathy sighed. "Then we'll have to take our chances with a medical doctor."

"I guess so."

"First thing's first: let's take care of the magical mess we're in now so you can move on to the close second."

"And what's that?"

"Telling your husband the truth."

CHAPTER 32

As soon as Samantha opened the door to their room, Steven came out to join them in the hall.

"It's about time!" he said. "Is everything okay?"

Kathy pushed past Samantha and stepped through the doorway. "You two can talk about that later. Right now, we need to borrow Scarlett for a bit again." She leaned into the guys' room and called, "Scarlett, can you come out here?"

"I want to talk about it now," Steven said, his eyes locked on Samantha.

Jeremy and Scarlett stepped out into the hall.

"Kathy, are we ever going to see each other this weekend?" Jeremy asked.

"Yes, we will," she said quickly, then turned to Scarlett. "The three of us need to talk."

"Are you sure we will?" Jeremy interjected. "Or am I going to spend the whole weekend with Steven?"

"I told you I needed to help Scarlett first."

"Is that why you pushed her off on us while you and Sam chitchatted alone?" He looked over at Scarlett and added, "No offense. It just doesn't add up."

She smiled and twirled a finger through her red curls.

"Sam and I just needed to discuss something first," Kathy said.

"And now I think it's time for *me* and her to talk," Steven said. "Sam, I don't like it that you're running ragged all over town. You looked exhausted. Go lay down and take a nap. All of this can wait."

"Steven, I have to help," Samantha said quietly.

"And it actually can't wait," Kathy added.

Steven put up his hand toward Kathy to shush her, then turned back to his wife. "You promised me that you'd slow down if I thought you needed a break."

Samantha held up a finger. "No, I didn't actually promise anything like that. You said you were only going to *try* to convince me. I never agreed to slow down at your whim. You know I have things I need to handle on my own."

"So what are you going to do, Sam?" Steven's voice grew, echoing down the hall. "Keep chasing after bad guys until you pass out again?"

"Bad guys?" Jeremy turned to Kathy with eyebrows raised. "Is that what you've been doing?"

"He's exaggerating," Kathy said quickly. "Shh."

Samantha shot daggers at Steven with her eyes, then turned and walked off down the hall.

Steven stood and watched her with his hands on his hips. After she had escaped into the elevator, he looked around at the rest of the group before pushing through and following after Samantha.

"At the risk of having the argument turn my way," Scarlett said in a soft voice, "maybe we should move this into one of the rooms before the other guests complain?"

"Good idea." Kathy ushered Jeremy and Scarlett into her room. She made sure to prop the door open for Samantha whenever she decided to return. Kathy didn't like the way Steven was acting, although if she were in his shoes, she might be just as concerned about Samantha. Still, it was best to remain a pair of listening ears to her sister while Steven pushed hard for her to see a doctor.

Inside, Jeremy took a seat on Kathy's bed. "So what are we doing now, then?"

Kathy paced at the foot of the beds, ignoring the fact that she had to squeeze around the cot to do so. "Well, maybe we can—"

Scarlett placed two fingers on Kathy's forehead, which made her instantly fall back onto the bed unconscious.

"Kathy!" Jeremy called, then turned to Scarlett. "What's going on?"

Scarlett smiled and stepped toward Jeremy, blocking his path to the door. He rose to his feet, but was blocked between the wall to the bathroom and the bed. Scarlett advanced toward him and he took several steps back until he couldn't.

"Hey lady, I don't know what you have in mind, but I just want to make it very clear that I'm only on this trip for Kathy."

Ignoring him, Scarlett smiled wider until she was inches away from him. "Finally, we're alone."

CHAPTER 33

- MAY 1986 -

"My sister is going to kill me if she ever finds out where I am tonight." Kathy walked beside Trisha in black pants and a jean jacket. They both wore heels, often reaching for each other to steady themselves. Being only nineteen, Kathy hadn't had a lot of occasion to wear them much, although she loved the way they looked.

"So just make sure she doesn't find out." Trisha fished in her purse for her lip gloss as she snapped her gum.

The two of them crossed the parking lot to the path leading to Ohio Hall at Penn State Behrend. Trisha's current boyfriend, Buzz, was a senior here and he and his roommate were having a party in the dorm while their resident assistant—or RA—was holing up in the library cramming for finals.

Buzz and his roommate had created a system, placing someone at a window on the second floor to watch for party guests, and a small group of "runners" to go down and sneak all of the guests in past the security guard. Every half hour, they rotated positions so that everyone could enjoy the party. They also had people coming and going from the library to check to make sure the RA was still there.

When the elevator dinged on the third floor, it opened up to a party happening in the lounge in the center of the two wings of the dorm building. There were couples making out on the few couches against the walls, others playing ping pong and air hockey, a group hung by the window to smoke. But the table with the booze was where most of the crowd was focused.

"Do you see Buzz?" Kathy asked Trisha over the music. Bon Jovi, "You Give Love a Bad Name."

Trisha shook her head, then suddenly grabbed Kathy's arm and pulled her down the hall toward one of the dorms. The music faded the further they traveled, but only slightly.

"This is his room here," Trisha said just before they stepped into the dorm.

There were bunk beds against one wall, two desks and wardrobes against the other, and a couch under the window.

There were people hanging out on both levels of the bed, the couch, and on the chairs to the desks. When the girls walked in, a blond guy with hair down to his ears stood up to greet them.

"Hey! You made it!" He wrapped Trisha in a hug, still

gripping his can of beer in his hand, and planted a kiss on her lips. Turning, he introduced them to the crowd. "Everyone, this is my girl, Trish. Trish, this is Kenny, Michael, Paul, Becky, Maddie, and Jeremy."

"And this is Kathy," Trisha added.

The group waved to them and the girls awkwardly waved back.

"Are you all seniors?" Kathy asked.

"Just me, Kenny, and Becky," Buzz said. "Maddie and Paul are juniors, and Jeremy and Michael are sophomores. But they're cool."

"Thanks for letting us in the club," Michael said with a laugh. "Sorry to ruin your rep."

"We had a regular game of pick-up football out on the quad," Jeremy said. "Guess we played good enough for Buzz and Kenny to want to be seen with us."

"You scored that touchdown to put that jackass Mitch in his place," Buzz said. "Of course you're good enough to hang." Turning back to the girls, he asked, "You ladies want a drink?"

Kathy put up her hand. "Oh no, I'm good."

"You sure?" he asked.

"We'll make sure you get home safe," Kenny added, a hint of a smile on his face. It said that they would think less of her if she didn't drink with the rest of them.

"No really, it's okay."

"I'll have one," Trisha said.

In her head, Kathy cursed her friend out, hoping that Trisha wouldn't drink too much. Or worse, lose her keys so that Kathy couldn't even drive them home. Samantha would *surely* kill Kathy if that happened.

As Buzz and Trisha disappeared back into the lounge, Kathy stood awkwardly by the door. Noticing, Jeremy stood up from his spot on the end of the couch near Maddie and Becky.

"Here, you can take my seat," he offered.

Kathy smiled, trying to remain polite, but the stress of Samantha potentially finding out about where she was, combined with the fact that Trisha was going to start drinking, made her feel too uncomfortable. "Actually, I, uh…I think I'm just going to go for a walk or something."

"Oh, come on!" Kenny shouted. "Stay! We won't bite."

"Hard," Michael added with a laugh.

Kathy rolled her eyes and turned to escape into the hall. Jeremy followed behind her.

"Do you mind if you have some company?" he asked.

"Huh?" she called back as they entered the lounge with the thumping music. The boombox was now playing Janet Jackson, "What Have You Done for Me Lately?"

Jeremy led her to an empty spot on the couch, receiving dirty looks from a couple at the drinks table. Probably because their spot had been stolen.

"I'm Jeremy," he said over the music.

"I know."

"You're Kathy?"

She nodded.

"How old are you?"

She considered lying, but knew that her age was likely obvious to all of these college kids. "Nineteen."

"Probably better that you don't drink." He set his own can of beer on the floor in front of the couch. "Bad habit."

She pointed to the group by the window. "Better than smoking."

"Now *that* I don't do," he said. "It just seems so gross."

She nodded. "So is this what it's like to be in college?"

"Has been for me," he said. "It's probably why my old man is getting me my own apartment next semester. Said I've been partying too much in the dorms." He waved his arms out to the rest of the crowd. "What better way to go out than to have a huge party?"

Kathy smiled at his defiance. Even if he wasn't the one who planned the party, he was making it known that he was here. And, truth be told, he seemed like one of the most sober people in the crowd. Certainly the cutest.

"Do you want to go downstairs to the lounge so we can talk without going hoarse?" he suggested.

A raspy voice would be a surefire way to tell her sister that she was somewhere a nineteen-year-old girl shouldn't have been. "Yes please."

He held out his hand and she placed hers in it without

thinking, like it came natural. He led her down the opposite hall and into a dank staircase that reeked of something fowl—Kathy tried not to think of what it was. Careful not to touch any of the handrails, she followed him down one flight of stairs to the second floor.

The music from the third floor was still present down here, but muffled. Kathy's ears rang a bit at the sudden relief.

"This is much better," he said.

"It is."

When they approached the empty second floor lounge, they took a seat on the couch, but Kathy didn't want to let go of his hand. She reached for it again when they sat. The two of them exchanged glances, then they both leaned in closer. Their lips touched briefly, and she pulled away to see his reaction.

A big, goofy grin was spread across her face, just like what was present on her own.

Going back in for another, she let him wrap his arms around her and they fell onto the couch with their lips locked together.

CHAPTER 34

Samantha made it down to the lobby of the hotel and stopped. She had no intention of stepping outside into the bitter February cold, but she needed space to clear her head. Instead, she settled for one of the black leather couches in the lobby, tucked away near a front window.

Just as she sat in the chair, she heard Steven call her name from across the lobby. She debated moving, but decided that that would only be childish. She had always prided herself on her ability to compromise and work things out in a relationship. Besides, they were married now and it's not like she could send him home to give them time to cool off.

"There you are." Steven stood over her with his hands on his hips. "Are you just going to give me the silent treatment?"

Samantha motioned to the seat across from her. "Sit. Let's talk."

He let out a heavy breath, but complied, leaning forward and resting his elbows on his knees. "I need you to be honest with me. How are you feeling?"

She was glad that the distance from the tension upstairs and the public space had put out his fuse, but she hated that the question persisted. Even though she could see it from his side, it annoyed her that he didn't trust her judgment of her own body.

"I'm still not feeling one hundred percent," she admitted, but raised her hand to stop his objections. "Regardless, I still have a job to do."

"If you're not feeling great, then you need to slow down."

"At first I thought it was just a headache," she said, ignoring his comment. "Then I thought it was something I ate or maybe a stomach bug, or something else entirely." She conveniently left out the word "pregnant." That had a tendency to perk up the ears of anyone, especially husbands. Worst of all, they hadn't discussed the possibility of kids at length and this was not the time or place to have that conversation. Especially since she knew that she *wasn't* pregnant. "Now I have no idea what it is. Honestly, it scares me a little."

Steven came over to sit beside her. He took ahold of her hand. "We need to go see a doctor."

She pulled her hand away and straightened up. "I'm not

dying. And even if I was, this weekend my first priority is to help Scarlett."

"Your first priority should always be to take care of your health."

"We only have a small window to help her," Samantha pushed. "I'm not going to miss it because I'm sick. I have a responsibility as a witch to help those in need."

"So you're refusing to go see a doctor?"

"For the time being, yes."

"That's stupid."

His words struck Samantha, but she tried not to show it. "I'm sorry you feel that way. But you knew who I was when you married me and I haven't changed."

"I know, Sam, but this is different," he said. "You're always in great health—or at least know what's making you sick. If you're passing out and having other episodes, then—"

"Other *episodes*?" she blurted, then withdrew her next words. This conversation was bordering on an argument again and she was not about to do that in a hotel lobby. She could tell the anger coming from Steven was partly due to the fact that she had pulled her hand away from him and wasn't obeying his wishes. But she was her own person. And she had never been one to back down from her responsibilities.

Another thing she prided herself on.

"I have a job to do," she said in an even tone. "If you can't accept that, then maybe we made a mistake getting married."

CHAPTER 35

Finally, we're alone." Scarlett pressed herself against Jeremy, wrapping her arms around him.

"Knock it off!" He had nowhere to go, being pinned between two walls and the bed. "What happened to Kathy? Why did she just pass out?"

Scarlett slipped one hand up the front of his shirt, while the other reached around for his butt.

"That's it!" He pushed at her, hard enough to make her stumble back a few steps. Seeing his only escape, her lunged across the bed, but she hopped on top of him.

"We can have a little fun while she's out." Scarlett squeezed her legs against his hips, pinning him. Meanwhile, she wrapped her hands in his, fighting to keep them steady.

"Kathy!" Jeremy called to her in the next bed. He struggled to push away at Scarlett's advances, but she was freakishly strong. "Kathy! Wake up and get this crazy broad off of me!"

Scarlett shimmied up his body, pinning his arms down with her knees. Jeremy frantically kicked with his legs, hoping to get enough traction on the bed or the wall or something to loosen her grip. But Scarlett held firm.

Grabbing ahold of his chin, she leaned forward to kiss him.

"What the hell is going on here?"

Jeremy and Scarlett both turned to look at Samantha, who had walked in without detection due to the open door.

Without wasting a moment, Samantha reached for Scarlett to pull her off. Once free, Jeremy stumbled over to the other bed to check on Kathy.

"What happened to her?" Samantha demanded of Scarlett, who struggled in her grip.

"What's with all the noise?" Steven asked as he entered. "I could hear you all the way down the—what's going on?"

"I'm trying to figure that out." Samantha looked at her husband and tried to plead with him to take Jeremy out of the room without saying anything—and certainly without using her power. Funny how moments ago they were having a heated conversation and now that were communicating without saying anything. Samantha was finding that marriage was full of ups and downs like that.

Steven seemed to catch on. "Come on, Jeremy, let's give the

girls some space."

"I'm not leaving her until she wakes up." Jeremy held Kathy's wrist to check for a pulse, meanwhile keeping his eyes on her chest to make sure she was breathing.

Scarlett rolled her eyes. "She'll wake up in a minute."

"I'll take care of her," Samantha assured him.

Steven stepped over and patted Jeremy on the shoulder, pushing him out across the hall toward their room. "It's probably just girl stuff. You don't want to hear about anymore of that than you need to."

When the door shut behind them, Samantha looked Scarlett in the eye and tried to probe her mind. With as annoyed as she was feeling, it didn't take long for Samantha to divert what was left of her energy toward the enchantress and determine there was a veil masking Scarlett's true intentions.

Releasing Scarlett, Samantha stepped back and said, "This is the spell that Ella put you under."

The distance from Jeremy seemed to dissipate the effects of the spell, but Samantha didn't want to take any chances.

"I think so too," Scarlett murmured. "It's all kind of…fuzzy."

Samantha wasn't the spell crafter of the two sisters, so the prospect of coming up with a counter spell for a spell she hadn't even heard recited the first time intimidated her. Still, she was empowered by the strength she had just felt with her telepathy. Maybe this was an opportunity for her to extend her capabilities in that area.

ENCHANTRESS

Probing into Scarlett's mind again, Samantha focused on the veil clouding Scarlett's mind. At first, she heard other errant thoughts: *What is she doing? What have I done to Kathy? Where is Oliver?*

All of these belonged to Scarlett. The fact that they weren't the thoughts of the people in the next room, or on the floors above or below them told Samantha that she was making progress with focusing this power. Scarlett was in the crosshairs, as she should be.

Taking it a step further, Samantha mentally swept away the spell coating Scarlett's mind and altering her thoughts. To Samantha, it was almost like shoveling snow, the way she cleaned up the effects of Ella's spell in Scarlett's mind.

Little by little, each bit of the spell cover was chipped away until there was nothing left but a tiny speck. Samantha figured that was the best she was going to do with her present capabilities. Luckily, it didn't seem to be a powerful spell.

Pulling out of Scarlett's head, Samantha sunk to the nearest bed. She was breathing heavy, feeling exhausted. She looked at the enchantress. "Feel any better?"

Scarlett shrugged. "I think."

Samantha sighed. "We'll have to keep you away from the guys until Kathy can wake up and officially reverse the spell. Or maybe Ella will, but I doubt she'll be cooperative. Now, what did you do to Kathy?"

"It's the same magic I used on you the other night," Scarlett said. "She should just be reliving the first time she met Jeremy."

"And she'll wake up on her own?"

Scarlett nodded.

Both of them stared at Kathy, who lay on the bed as if she were asleep. Yet she didn't stir at all.

The more the minutes ticked away, the more doubtful Samantha became that Scarlett was telling the truth. Were the effects of the spell still present in Scarlett? Was this just a trick to stall for time? What spell had *really* been cast on Kathy? Samantha wondered if she should've been more skeptical of Scarlett from the beginning. She really was off of her A-game.

Finally, Kathy opened her eyes. She groaned and stretched, then sat up with a smile. Suddenly noticing Samantha and Scarlett, she said, "Oh. Hello. What did I miss?"

CHAPTER 36

What did you miss?" Samantha asked. "Let's see, the spell that Ella put on Scarlett finally revealed itself and she nearly took advantage of your maybe-boyfriend."

Kathy shot Scarlett a look, who turned away bashfully.

"I'm sorry," Scarlett said. "It is a moment I am ashamed of."

When Kathy turned back to her sister, Samantha said, "I took care of it. For now, at least. But I think it's a good idea to keep Scarlett away from the guys until we can get to Ella."

"Okay," Kathy said.

"What did you see?" Scarlett asked. "I didn't cause you to live out some horrible nightmare, did I?"

"Not at all! I was reliving the moment I met Jeremy. That first night at that party in his dorm room. How we—"

"His *dorm room*?" Samantha cut in. "*That's* where you met him? You told me you ran into him at the diner!"

Kathy bit her lip. "I did say that, didn't I?"

Samantha gave her sister a disappointing look, but let it slide for the moment. She took a deep breath, feeling her energy creep back with each passing minute. "Anyway. The fact that Ella put a spell on Scarlett means she's trying to distract us from something. So we need to regroup quickly before she can pull off whatever it is she's trying to do."

"Do you think she ran away and took Oliver in that hourglass with her?" Scarlett asked. "She's had enough time."

"Maybe, but I don't think so," Samantha said. "If anything, I think that Ella thinks that she's won and now she's celebrating. But I'm sure she has back-up insurances just in case." She took another big breath. "Besides, I think that maybe she's about to free Oliver from the hourglass. Which means that we won't have to."

"Are you sure you're okay?" Kathy asked.

"I'm *fine*," Samantha groaned.

Kathy put up her hands in surrender. "Okay. Just checking. Anyway, why do you think that she's freed Oliver? She's had him trapped for almost a year. Why would she let him out of the bottle now?"

"You're right, she has had him for a year, but I don't think she's freed him just yet," Samantha explained. "She probably knew that Scarlett would return someday and she had no idea when that would be. She didn't want to be taken by surprise."

"She's been living in fear of the unknown," Scarlett murmured.

"Exactly. But now she thinks she's successfully thwarted Scarlett," Samantha said. "If the theory stands true and the effects of Ella's spell will be permanent after a year, Ella probably thinks that when she boards the bus tomorrow back for New York City, there will be enough time that's passed that Scarlett won't be able to catch up to her."

"But why free Oliver?" Kathy asked. "Why not just wait until she's back in New York?"

Samantha raised her eyebrows at her sister. "Think about your own temptations. Ella's literally had Oliver in her pocket for the last year but has been afraid of releasing him. Now the fear's gone but the temptation remains. I can't imagine she's going to want to wait any longer. And if he's freed, we can use the location ritual again to find him."

"So we'll use her own lust against her," Scarlett said.

"Exactly."

"Of course, that's all assuming your theory is right, Sam, and she's freed Oliver," Kathy added. "What if she still has him hidden somewhere?"

"That's what we'll find out when we find her."

"Next question: where the hell is she?"

Again, Samantha gave her sister a look. "Put yourself in Ella's shoes. If you've had the hots for some guy and have been anticipating spending a night with him for a year, where do you think you'd be?"

Kathy blushed a little. "Ella's in her hotel room."

"I know which hotel the show usually books," Scarlett said. "But how are we going to know where Ella's room is? The front desk won't tell us, and if I'm spotted by anyone in the crew, it might cause a scene. That might just give Ella enough time to run away or cast another spell."

Samantha smirked. "I have a plan for that."

CHAPTER 37

Samantha led Kathy down the hall of yet another floor at the hotel on Delaware and Chippewa. The sisters were quiet as Samantha focused on her power. Like a radar, she tried to cast a wide net to pick up on the thoughts of the people in the rooms she passed. She thought that she'd be able to distinguish Ella's thoughts apart from the others. So far the experiment was just adding to her headache.

When will Doris get back?

Does room service deliver in the middle of the day?

I hope my wife doesn't figure out I'm here.

The endless stream of thoughts invaded Samantha's mind and just as quickly faded from it as she moved down the hall. Yet another sign that she was getting a better grip on this new ability of hers, but offering nothing in the way of clues to lead to Ella and Oliver.

Worse, the persistent use of her power was dragging her down. Each step seemed harder than the last. But she needed to push through it for Scarlett's sake.

"Anything?" Kathy whispered.

Samantha put a finger to her lips, but shook her head. She turned around the corner and was bombarded with even more thoughts, these ones closer to what she was looking for.

I should have time to check out the gym before the bus leaves tomorrow.

Can't wait to get home.

This movie sucks.

So glad to have a day off.

Finally, I have him to myself.

Samantha put up her hand to signal to Kathy. They had stopped outside the door where Samantha had heard that last thought. She listened for more.

I hope there's no long-term damage to him after being trapped for so long. Maybe I can cast a spell to fix him and make him forget about Scarlett.

Nodding, Samantha pointed to the door.

Kathy stepped forward to initiate the plan they had discussed. Meanwhile, Samantha hurried back down the hall and toward the lobby, where Scarlett was waiting. She was grateful for no longer needing to use her power.

As Scarlett had warned, if she was seen by one of the cast or crew members, it would draw unwanted attention to them and the whole plan would be ruined. It was better for Scarlett to wait downstairs. Kathy would stand guard outside Ella's room and freeze them if they came out before Samantha returned.

When Samantha joined Scarlett in the lobby, the two women exchanged brief glances. As Samantha casually passed by Scarlett to take her seat by the window, she muttered, "Room 515."

Scarlett offered a subtle nod and continued toward the front desk, where a handsome man in a brown sports jacket stood working at a computer.

Samantha wasn't too familiar with computers. She'd used them a bit in college here and there, and Mr. Marsden had one at work for the office files, but for the most part they were still a mystery to her. Maybe someday she'd be able to get some more experience with one.

From across the lobby, Samantha watched as Scarlett flirted with the desk clerk. Smiling wide, twisting her red curls, and laughing along with everything the man said. And, Samantha was sure, a little magic pheromones to increase the man's interest in her.

Within five minutes, the man had disappeared into the office behind the desk. Scarlett turned and gave Samantha a thumbs up and the witch started making her way to the elevators. She waited until Scarlett had secured the key and the two stepped into the open elevator and waited for the doors to close.

"You got the key to Ella's room?" Samantha asked.

Scarlett nodded. "And I didn't even need to flash my boobs."

The witch turned to her with wide eyes.

"It's not like I do it *often*," Scarlett said. "Just when I have to."

Samantha shook her head with a grin. It was almost like talking to Kathy.

When the door opened on the fifth floor, Samantha pointed down the hall. "They're in a room just up here."

When they rounded the corner, Kathy waved them toward her. "Hurry! She's got Oliver out, but I think I heard her cast a spell on him. Not sure what it did, but we still need to be careful. He might not be acting like himself—and we may need Ella to reverse the spell."

Samantha took the key from Scarlett and quickly opened the lock. Scarlett brushed past her and burst into the room with Kathy on her heels.

Oliver was pinned to the bed beneath Ella, much like Jeremy had been with Scarlett only a few hours earlier back at their hotel.

"Get off of him!" Scarlett shouted.

"How did you—" Before Ella finished her sentence, the enchantress had pulled her off the bed and threw her to the floor. As Ella attempted to get up, Kathy put up her hands and froze the witch.

"That should hold her for a few minutes," she said. "But how are we going to remove the spell on Oliver?"

"Oliver." Scarlett cradled his face in her hands. Her voice quivered with emotion as she was reunited with her lover. "Sweetie, it's me. Scarlett. I've missed you so much. Please look at me."

But Samantha only saw a blank expression on Oliver's face. He seemed to be more focused on the ceiling than Scarlett.

"You didn't freeze him, did you?" Samantha asked her sister.

"No, just Ella."

Leaning forward, the enchantress planted a kiss on Oliver's lips, holding it for several seconds for good measure. When she pulled away, all three women waited for something to happen, but Oliver remained the same.

"So much for true love's kiss," Kathy said.

"What do we do?" Scarlett asked the sisters. Her voice was raw with emotion.

Pulling a small vial out of her pocket, Samantha stepped toward Ella. "I prepared this potion just in case."

"What kind of potion?" Kathy asked.

"A power-stripping potion."

"And that will remove the spell from Oliver?" Scarlett asked.

Samantha nodded. "It should remove her magic and any spell she's cast with it."

"Wait, Sam." Kathy reached for her sister's arm to stop her. "Are you sure about this?"

"Why not?" Samantha asked. "She's frozen. Her mouth is open enough for me to pour the potion inside. She'll swallow enough for it to take effect. It's the perfect moment, and we're running out of time."

"But taking away a witch's powers? Doesn't that seem…wrong?"

Samantha motioned to the man sprawled out on the bed. "And what she's done to Oliver—and Scarlett—for the last year isn't wrong?"

"Not to sound too much like an after-school special, but two wrongs don't make a right," Kathy said. "Are we sure this is justified?"

"It's better than killing her."

"That's a low bar to set."

"What other choices do we have?"

Kathy looked between Ella, Oliver, and Scarlett. Finally, she shrugged. "I guess we don't have any others."

Samantha paused for a moment to be sure there were no other objections, then popped the cork from the vial and poured the contents down Ella's throat. "Unfreeze her. We have to make sure she swallows it."

She tossed the vial aside and knelt down beside Ella, preparing herself for a struggle.

With the flick of her hand, Kathy reversed her magic and Ella came springing back to life. This time, she began choking on the potion.

Samantha was quick, clamping her hand under Ella's chin and wrestling her on the floor. Ella frantically squirmed, but Samantha held her grip.

"You don't deserve your powers if you're going to misuse them," Samantha told her between ragged breaths. "We're supposed to serve and protect, not manipulate for our own benefit."

Samantha watched as Ella reluctantly took a gulp of the potion along with a frantic gasp for air. She erupted into coughs with some of the potion seeping from her lips and between Samantha's fingers. Still, the witch kept her hand clamped on Ella's chin and over her mouth.

"Oliver!" Scarlett cried in the commotion.

"Scarlett?"

The sound of Oliver's voice told Samantha that her potion had taken effect on Ella. With that assurance, she released her.

Ella remained on the floor and coughed. She cast a venomous look at Samantha. "You might think you're high and mighty, but you just proved you're not much different than me."

"I didn't trap someone against their will for a year," Samantha said.

"But you took my powers away against mine."

Kathy put her hand on her sister's shoulder. "Sam, I think we should go while we still have the upper hand."

Samantha rose to her feet and wiped the hand that had

been covered Ella's mouth on her jeans. "Yeah. We've done what we came to do."

The sisters turned to Scarlett and Oliver, who were locked in an embrace. While Samantha could see the smile on Kathy's face, Samantha felt saddened by their desire for one another.

Thanks to Scarlett's vision, she knew there was a time when she and Steven had felt that spark for each other. Lately, though, that spark seemed to be gone.

Was her marriage doomed already?

CHAPTER 38

I had a dream about you."

Jeremy's face lit up at that, looking almost heavenly in the glow from the candlelight on the table. "You did, did you?"

Kathy rolled her eyes. "It was more about *us*. More like a memory."

He reached for his glass of beer and took a sip. "Mm-hmm."

"About the time we first met." She stabbed her fork into her salmon, hoping to mask any embarrassment that might come if he didn't reciprocate the sentiment. "Do you remember that?"

Jeremy sat back and thought about it. Kathy watched him with warmth. They had managed to extend their weekend—last minute calls into work and Kathy skipping a couple classes—so they could spend Valentine's Day together. Although, neither of them had acknowledged the holiday, even if that was the reason for the extension.

"Would you like to stay a few extra days and leave Wednesday morning?" Jeremy had asked her.

"I could use a long weekend," Kathy had said.

Both of them knew what that meant, but their reunion was still fairly new. And as much as Kathy tried to forget, her few encounters with Lisa haunted her like an unwanted ghost. She tried not to think about what Jeremy had told her about his spontaneous trip to Buffalo with his ex.

Still, it was worth it to Kathy to spend a few days alone with Jeremy in an uninterrupted bubble of time. It was like the two of them had stepped into an alternate reality where all of their responsibilities were pushed aside and they were only focused on each other. That was something they desperately needed. Even if Kathy was going to pay for the fact that she was missing work and classes. And Jeremy was sure to be in for an uncomfortable conversation with Lisa in some way.

"The first time we met," Jeremy said, bringing Kathy back to the present, "was my last semester staying in the dorms."

"Right!"

"Buzz and Kenny had that huge party. And you and I escaped downstairs and talked on the couch."

Kathy looked down at her food. "Among other things."

He smiled. "We hit it off pretty quickly."

"That's what I was thinking too. It all came so naturally. We had a connection right away."

"I'd like to think we still do." He reached across the table for her hand and she gave it to him. "That's why we…*reconnected* the way we did."

"And we haven't *reconnected* like that since."

He gave her hand a quick squeeze. "Hopefully that will change soon. When the time's right."

Kathy had splurged and kept the room she shared with Samantha and Scarlett when they first arrived. Scarlett had went to stay with Oliver, and Samantha and Steven went home. Kathy insisted that Jeremy keep the guys' room too, so they could keep *some* lines drawn until they had discussed their relationship.

Up until now, they'd been preoccupied with exploring the city and having fun. Reconnecting in a more natural way. It was nice, almost nostalgic.

"These last few days have meant a lot to me," Kathy said. "I almost hate to see it come to an end."

"I know. But we can't keep living this fairytale life for long. We have to do boring things, like go to work."

She laughed. "Boring, but necessary." Taking in a deep breath, she bit the bullet and spoke what had been on her mind all weekend. "Honestly, I think we're worth a second shot. I'd love to see where it takes us again, but—"

"Lisa."

"Yeah."

"She and I have made no promises to each other," he said.

"She deserves an explanation, of course, but as far as I'm concerned, she's not standing in our way."

Kathy pulled her hand back and resumed stabbing at her food. "Yeah, you mentioned that before."

"What bothers me, Kathy, is the way you passed out on Saturday."

She looked at him, confused. "Passed out?"

"When your friend almost—well, she jumped me!"

"Oh. That. That was nothing."

Jeremy studied her. "Weren't you telling me the other day how worried you were about Samantha because she doesn't know what's wrong with her?"

Kathy cringed. That was a late-night discussion where she revealed a lot of things, like how she sometimes felt like a misfit compared to her sister or that she wasn't sure if she was suited for college. Things that she thought would be locked away in the memory of that night and never spoken of again.

"That's different."

"How?"

"Sam passed out at work. I…" Kathy paused, only briefly, to search for a good excuse. "I just didn't have enough to drink that day. And I hadn't slept well the night before on the hotel mattress."

"You've slept just fine ever since."

"It must've been from the trip up here, then."

He looked at her and she could tell he didn't believe her.

After all, it *was* a lie, but she couldn't exactly tell him the truth, either.

"I'm fine, Jeremy," she assured him. "Really. I've slept—and felt—great ever since."

Picking at his fries, he muttered, "Okay."

"I appreciate the concern, though."

His eyes snapped up to meet hers. "Of course. You mean a lot to me, Kathy. And if I haven't made it abundantly clear by now, let me just state it plainly: I want to give us another shot."

Kathy smiled and reached for his hand again. "I'd like that too. But what about Lisa?"

"I'll straighten it out with her when we get back to Erie."

"I don't want to break up a relationship."

"She and I don't have a relationship," he promised. "We were just hanging out, hitting it off a bit, sure. But it's nothing compared to what I feel when I'm with you, Kathy. I know you've probably dated other people since we broke up. I'm not crazy about that, but I can't hold it against you either. We've gotta move forward. And I want to move forward with you."

Kathy squeezed his hand and the two of them leaned over the table to share a kiss. Even though she'd been down this road before with him, this time felt different. They were both different.

Maybe this time, things would finally work between them.

CHAPTER 39

The evening hadn't turned out to be the romantic Valentine's Day dinner that Samantha had hoped it would be. Their first one as a married couple came with tension and an awkwardness that hadn't existed before.

Well, maybe only during that time when she had told him she was a witch. But even that was different.

"Thanks for making dinner," she offered as she picked at her chicken.

"Of course, but you have to help me with the dishes."

"Okay."

They sat alone in the dining room at home. The smell of the roasted chicken wafted through the house. There were several candles lit in the dining room, offering a warm glow. A fire crackled in the living room, but Samantha wasn't sure if they would get to enjoy it tonight.

Usually they celebrated an empty house as date night. Tonight, she feared, that prospect was already ruined long before it even had a chance.

They had been fumbling around each other ever since they got back home on Sunday. Samantha wasn't sure if Steven was annoyed with her about her responsibilities as a witch taking precedence over her health, or if he was still annoyed that she quickly turned down his idea to get their own place. She thought he might be happy having a few days alone without Kathy, but neither of them seemed to be.

Finally, Steven set his fork down and said, "Sam, I'm sorry for arguing with you this past weekend."

So that was what was bothering him. She had resisted the temptation to read his mind to figure out what it was. It was a relief to finally hear it out loud. And the fact that it started with an apology on his part was a perk.

"You were just worried about me," she said. "I get it."

"What *I* don't get is why you put being a witch over taking care of yourself," he said. "But I suppose I married an independent person who was a witch long before I ever knew you, so I can't control you."

"Thank you."

They were quiet again. The apology was an olive branch, but it didn't fix the stress between them. Maybe they needed time to deal with it. Or maybe they needed concrete answers that neither of them had. If they knew that Samantha had a fever or a cold or the flu or something else that could be treated, she figured things wouldn't be so awkward between them. It was the unknown that was causing all of this.

"I'll consider seeing a doctor if I don't feel any better by the end of the week," she offered. Even without reading his mind, she knew that's what he was thinking. "I haven't had anymore episodes or anything since we've been home. A mild headache and some queasiness, but nothing as bad as last week. A few more days can't hurt."

Steven sighed heavily. "I wish you'd go sooner. What if it's serious?"

The tears on her face surprised even Samantha, but they rushed out of her unexpectedly. "That's it." Her voice cracked. "What if it is serious?"

He shot out of his seat and came around the table to sit beside his wife, wrapping his arm around her shoulder. "Hey, it's okay. We'll get through it together."

Samantha wiped at her tears and leaned into Steven's chest. It was just the two of them, so she allowed herself to fall apart. Honesty was one of the strengths of their relationship. "I guess I'm just scared. My mom died young. I don't want that to be me. I don't want to die before I've had a chance to really live."

"Hey, no one's dying." He squeezed her tight, which helped. She hadn't realized how much she'd been missing his hug, his affection, until he offered it again. "As long as I'm around, I'm going to do everything I can to protect you."

Samantha loved that he wanted to, but she wasn't sure if he even could.

Suspecting she might be pregnant, Samantha seeks out Vanita, an oracle, to ask whether she and Steven are even ready to have kids. During the reading, Samantha receives a vision of a man bleeding out on the ground. Learning from past mistakes, Samantha recruits Kathy's help to track him down.

After searching for hours in the frigid winter night, the sisters come up empty. Samantha returns to Vanita for further answers and learns that the man in the vision is none other than Vanita's brother, Oren. When the sisters enact their plan to save Oren, they discover that Vanita isn't as innocent as she let on. Right in front of the sisters' eyes, she stabs her brother and steals her family's powerful amulet to wreak havoc with it.

The sisters are ready to launch into a search for Vanita, but must tend to Oren's physical injuries, as well as some of their own intangible ones as Kathy finds Steven in a compromising situation, which erupts in the biggest marital spat he and Samantha have ever had. The sisters must pull together their emotions and trust each other if they're going to get the amulet back. Otherwise, the world as they know it could be over.

Oracle is the seventh book in the Coven series, which serves as a prequel to the Under the Moon series.

ORACLE

COVEN: BOOK 7

Read on for an excerpt of the next book in
the Coven series!

DAVID NETH

CHAPTER 1

- MAY 1983 -

The gardens were beautifully laid out in between the old mansions. It was such a wide lot that Oren wondered if there had once been a house standing where the gardens now lay or if the original builder of the mansion had always intended this lot to be used for nature's beauty.

Not that Oren was here to admire the flora. He had a much sinister intention.

It was the traditional end-of-the-semester celebration that the head of the history department threw for his students. As fun and generous as it appeared on the outside, it was also obvious that the professor certainly liked to be praised for his material possessions—whatever powered his ego.

Oren walked up the brick pathway from the sidewalk and

through the iron gate into the garden. The beauty of the yard was hidden behind large bushes. The professor wanted people to admire his property, but only when he invited them and only when he could hear their praises.

College students milled about, drinking cocktails, even though most of them probably weren't even old enough. Their chatter revolved around finals, moving out of the dorms, and summer plans. Few of them discussed career prospects greater than summer employment at Mike's Mini Mart and Gas Station.

The gardens were symmetrically squared off, with brick pathways framing four prominent flower gardens. Beyond, there was a small open grassy area beneath a large mature oak tree with a pergola that matched the same colors as the ornate brick house.

Oren made his way back to the pergola, where the drinks table was set up. He fixed himself a martini as he listened to the conversations behind him. It was imperative to find where the professor was before the professor found him.

Sipping the smallest of sips so as to keep a level head, Oren stood casually in the shade with one hand in his pocket and the other clutching his drink. He surveyed the yard and saw cliques of people grouped together in conversation.

Nobody appeared to be in the house at first. And then, Oren watched as a particularly inebriated young man nearly tripped down the brick steps when he exited the sunroom in his pursuit back to the drinks table. Oren saw a face in the porcelain throne in the young man's future.

Still, the access to the sunroom gave him an idea. Surely, it wasn't enough for the professor to idly accept praise for his house. No, he would want to encourage it by offering tours to students who would do any amount of sucking up to get a better grade on their final assignments.

Setting his drink on the table, Oren walked with purpose to the sunroom, anticipating questioning looks that never came.

Inside, the professor was finishing up a tour with a small group of students. He laughed and thanked the group for their comments and looks of wonder. Despite the casual nature of the party, the professor wore dark blue dress pants and a white button-down shirt. Most prominent of all was the red amulet that hung around his neck. It caught the light coming in from the windows in the sunroom and cast the space with bright red light.

"Thank you, thank you," he said, adjusting his perfectly-rolled sleeves on his biceps. "Yes, I am quite proud of my home. I'm certainly glad that you enjoy it as well." He noticed Oren and the smile deflated just a smidgen. Turning back to his students, he cranked up the strength of his smile and said, "Why don't you all go out and enjoy the gardens and, if you're old enough, a beverage?"

The group moved toward the door, ignoring Oren. The professor held the door open for them, then closed it behind them. With a flick, he locked it.

"I was wondering when I would see you again," he said with his back to Oren.

"You certainly didn't think that I wouldn't come for what is mine."

The professor turned and smiled at Oren. "What is yours? I acquired the amulet fairly."

"It was theft."

In his breast pocket, the professor reached for a pipe. "Mind if I have a smoke? I have a feeling that this will be a stressful conversation, although I'm confident that we can come to an agreement."

Oren motioned for him to continue, then looked around the room. "You know, I've been looking into you since you first entered my life. I'm intrigued by the fact that you've worked your way into high society."

"High society?" the professor asked, taking a puff of his pipe.

"You teach history at Gannon University. You have a stately address and a beautifully restored home. You have people fanning all over you."

The professor smiled, playing at bashfulness. "Well, yes, in that way I suppose you can say I am part of high society."

"You crave power of all kinds," Oren went on. "Academically, financially, socially…magically."

At that, the professor's head snapped up to Oren. "You think you're clever, don't you?"

"Not clever. Truthful."

"And what, may I ask, is your version of the truth?"

"My version is the only truth: you stole my family's amulet in your thirst for power."

"You see, that's not—"

"I want it back." It was painful enough to Oren for having lost it. But seeing it around another man's neck—someone who had no right to wear it—infuriated Oren.

"I'm afraid that is simply not going to happen." The professor pulled the pipe from his teeth and waved it at Oren. A streak of lightning shot from the end of the pipe and struck the plaster beneath the staircase behind Oren.

"I do not want to harm you, but you leave me no choice," the professor said.

"You've never hesitated to harm anyone before." Oren threw a small vial at the base of the professor's feet, which sent up a cloud of smoke in his face, making him cough. Oren raced forward, but was intercepted with a force so strong that it lifted him upward and across the large entry room.

The professor stepped out of the magical smoke and toward Oren, who scrambled back to his feet. The professor grabbed the front of Oren's shirt and forced him to his feet, pushing him against the wall.

"And to think, I didn't even need to use your family's amulet," he said. "That would be the just desserts you deserve, wouldn't it?"

ORACLE

The latch on the sunroom door jangled and a student knocked on the glass. The professor turned toward the noise. Oren didn't waste any time. He pulled the knife from his belt and drove it straight through the heart of the professor.

Immediately, Oren was drenched in the professor's blood. The clutch on his shirt loosened as the professor fell to the floor. The student behind the glass screamed as she watched the attack.

Oren needed to act quickly.

Snatching the amulet from around the professor's neck, he bolted to the front door and out onto the street. He ran without looking back. Even though the sorcerer had pushed him to murder—something he swore he would never do—it felt right. At the very least, he got justice for his family's loss.

CHAPTER 2

- FEBRUARY 1989 -

Samantha stepped out of the clinic into the gloomy, cold weather. She pulled her coat around her tighter and beelined for her car.

As much as she tried to downplay Steven's concerns about her health—she hoped that he would forget it altogether—she knew he wouldn't. And he hadn't so far. Which, she ultimately knew, was a good thing to have a husband care about you so much that they insist you go to the doctor when things are wrong. But it was annoying at times.

Samantha would rather not have taken the afternoon off simply to get blood work done, several days before her actual doctor appointment. She had the time, but it was still her first year. And in her industry, they were well into their busy season: tax season.

Samantha blasted the heat once she got to her car and glanced at the time. It was just after two. Too late to go back to work, but if she went home she'd feel guilty about being home, feeling as though she should be working instead. A bad mindset to have, she knew, but it was how she felt. She was a workaholic.

As she navigated her car out of the parking lot and onto Liberty Street, she decided at the last minute to turn right instead of left, swerving into the opposite lane, where an oncoming car down the street got nervous and beeped at her. She managed to swing back into her lane long before the other car passed.

Worry wart.

When she pulled up to the stop light at West 32nd Street, reality set in. That wasn't a safe thing to do and wasn't like her. Maybe there *was* something wrong with her.

In truth, she had only felt marginally better since she'd promised Steven to go see the doctor last week on Valentine's Day. Maybe getting checked out wasn't such a terrible thing. Still, she was worried about what the doctors might uncover.

Since she'd feel guilty going home, Samantha reasoned that she'd feel more accomplished with her time off if she was running errands. She turned left onto West 26th Street, drove several blocks down the overbuilt street, then sat in the shared turning lane waiting for traffic to pass so she could pull into the parking lot of the Apothecary.

It was an herbal shop she had discovered a couple weeks ago—one where she had certainly left an impression. One that she wanted to help clear up by frequenting it.

When she walked in, the woman behind the counter smiled at her as she recognized her.

"Welcome back," she said with a bright smile and a wave.

Samantha nodded. "Hello Margaret. How are you?"

"Not too bad." She came over from the cart of herb plants by the window with a watering can in her hand. "What can I do for you?"

"Actually, I came in to stock up on some herbs. I have a list here. Would you mind checking?" Samantha handed her a slip of paper from her grocery notepad.

Margaret set the watering can down on the floor. "No problem at all. I'll be right back." She stepped to the far wall and Samantha busied herself by looking through the rest of the items in the shop.

The Apothecary was different than Mystic Treasures, the other occult shop that she and Kathy usually frequented in Erie. The Apothecary had authentic magical instruments and ingredients, but they were limited. The stock was overpowered by novelty gimmicks like spirit stones and scented candles and wind chimes that alluded to the otherworldly, but didn't explicitly embrace it. Still, the shop offered enough of the basics that it wasn't a wasted trip.

"Hey Margaret," Samantha started.

"Hmm?" She tilted her head up toward Samantha, her focus still on the stock of herbs.

"You wouldn't happen to have any recommendations for, uh…fortune tellers or seers or oracles or someone like that, would you?"

Samantha had tried to consult with one several weeks ago before she really started to feel ill. But then several magical emergencies popped up, as well as the newlywed spats she'd been having with Steven, and finding the answer to the question that had been bothering her took a back seat.

The question got Margaret's attention. "Well, I don't know. You know, Laurie has a list of what she calls *specialists* in a notebook under the register, but I haven't looked too hard at it. I thought that it was quite silly, but I can check if you're interested."

"If you could."

"Absolutely." Margaret set the final jar of dried herbs in a basket along with the others she had collected and stepped back to the register. She pulled the book out and began to flip through. "Hmm…let's see here. Um…"

Samantha looked down at the book and did her best to read upside down. "Preferably someone who isn't just going to con me out of my money."

"Oh, of course," Margaret said with a fervent nod. She flipped through absently, clearly not really understanding the list.

Shamans, witch doctors, ghost hunters. From what Samantha could read, the list was very much like the shop: authentic, yet disguised by gimmicks.

"Wait," Samantha called out suddenly. "What's that?" She put her finger down to the woman who had the title "oracle" listed beside her.

"Vanita Patel," Margaret read. "It says here she has a shop on Parade Street. On the corner of 11th."

"Perfect, do you mind jotting that down? You can just add it to the bottom of my list there."

Margaret transcribed the information, cashed Samantha out, and bid her farewell. Samantha stepped back out into the cold and looked down at the address. Was she desperate enough to see an oracle?

Then again, she had done crazier things in the last few weeks. She started the car and merged back into traffic.

Parade and 11th were across town, but Samantha didn't mind the drive. Fifteen minutes later, she pulled into a parking spot on the street in front of a row of houses that had been converted to commercial buildings a long time ago. They had seen better days.

The whole area, in fact, had the feel of vacant prosperity. Empty buildings, vacant lots of businesses torn down for crumbling parking lots. It wasn't the best image of Erie and it made Samantha nervous of what she was going to walk into. But it was the middle of the day and there was no one outside.

Maybe this Vanita lady wasn't even open.

Samantha stepped through the door of the small storefront on the first floor of the converted house. Inside, there was no remnant of a residential dwelling.

Red velvet curtains hung on the walls. Purple and gold patterned fabric hung from pins on the ceiling, sectioning off the sad looking waiting area from whatever lay in the back. The room smelled of incense and mildew. The whole atmosphere summoned up an image of this Vanita woman in Samantha's mind and it wasn't someone she wanted to meet for real.

Samantha turned and had her hand on the door in an attempt to escape when she heard someone behind her say, "Oh, hello. Are you here for a reading?"

No way to retreat now.

Turning, Samantha smiled. "Yes, sorry. I wasn't sure you were open."

"Nonsense, I'm here. I'm open. Come on back."

Vanita wasn't as bad as Samantha had imagined. For one, she had all her teeth, it seemed. She had her curly dark hair tucked up on her head with a series of bright colored headbands. Despite the damp chill in the room, she wore a T-shirt and a flowing skirt that matched the fabric holding her hair.

Samantha followed Vanita behind the curtain, where a wooden table sat in the center of the room. To the left was clearly the oracle's chair, as it was surrounded by boxes of trinkets, as well as magazines and newspapers and bottles of water. The other chair was a standard office chair.

"Have a seat."

Samantha set her purse on her lap and sat on the edge of the chair. She unwound her scarf, pulled off her gloves, and extended her hand. "I'm Samantha—"

Vanita threw up her hands. "Don't tell me! And don't touch me!" She laughed. "I know I sound—and probably *look*—crazy, but I try to start everyone's reading with a clean slate."

Samantha smiled politely. "Okay."

She narrowed her eyes and studied Samantha. "Hmm…you're obviously very independent, judging by the way you carry yourself and the fact that you're here alone. I don't think you're an only child, but I do suspect you're the oldest of your siblings. I'm sensing a lot of responsibility on your part, which speaks to your independence, so that makes sense."

Samantha was impressed. These weren't generalities like some so-called fortune tellers sprouted. These were specific— and correct—key points about her as a person.

"You're young, but not inexperienced. I'm guessing that you've already had to work for a lot in your life, so there is a touch of pride. However, you still have some drive because there's a lot more you want to do. And I'm also assuming you hold high standards for yourself, so you don't just settle for good enough. How am I doing?"

Smiling, Samantha said, "That was amazing. Dead on. Are you…are you, um…*gifted*?" She didn't know how to ask the "magic" question in case Vanita had just gotten lucky—or simply cheated somehow.

The oracle laughed. "Yes, honey, I'm magical. As are you."

"Right." It felt awkward to admit that, but clearly Vanita already knew it as soon as Samantha had walked through the door. Was there something about her that said, "Witch"?

"So what can I do for you, dear?"

"Well…I just got married—"

"Congratulations!" Vanita beamed.

Samantha smiled again. "Thanks. Anyway, my husband brought up the question of kids, and with…what I do, I'm just not sure that's such a good idea."   Vanita tapped her chin with her finger. "I see. Well, let's get a reading set up then." She dug through the boxes beside her chair, pulling out candles, incense, altar cloths, mirrors, the whole nine yards.

"You don't need to know more?" Samantha watched as Vanita spread the altar cloth out and arranged the candles on the table. She got to her feet and positioned the mirror to reflect the dim sunlight coming from the front window.

"No, dear," she said as she worked. "The reading is for you. You will see what you need to see. I'm simply the channel for the message."

"Interesting. But don't you read fortunes too?"

Vanita bent over behind the table and pulled out a lighter. She flicked it several times, igniting the incense until it began to smoke. "I do that when the client is not sure what they want to see. As I've already determined, you are very driven. You know what you want. We won't have any issues here."

She set the incense on the floor and sat back down. Stretching her arms across the table, she motioned for Samantha to take her hands, which she did.

"Concentrate on the question you want answered," Vanita instructed. "Forget everything else. Try to relax. Take deep breaths."

Samantha tried, but the incense made it hard to fill her lungs with fresh air. And the reflection from the mirror shining in her face made it hard to concentrate. But she kept her eyes closed and her hands in Vanita's.

Foreign words spewed out of Vanita's mouth and she gripped Samantha's arms with surprising strength. Samantha resisted the temptation to open her eyes and see what was happening, but then she felt her mind escaping her. As if she were lifting out of her body.

In a flash, she was struck with a vision. A dark alley at night time. A man lay in blood-covered snow, clutching what looked to be a fatal wound in his side.

Just as quickly as it came, it was gone. Samantha pulled away from Vanita and gasped.

"Well, *that* was unexpected," Vanita said.

Samantha snatched up her purse, her gloves, her scarf, and started toward the door. "I'm sorry, but I have to go."

Why did this keep happening to her?

CHAPTER 3

Kathy raced to the register. She had clocked in *just* in time and needed to be on the sales floor immediately. She felt like she'd been running from one thing to the next all day.

"Girl, where's the fire?" Leslie folded some of the returns on the second register.

"My bus was running late and I could only walk so fast across the parking lot, because heaven forbid the mall salts the sidewalks." Kathy snapped her name tag on her shirt. Afterwards, she straightened everything and checked to make sure the buttons lined up correctly. The store required her to wear the latest fashions to advertise to the customers, and her outfit—a nice blouse and black pants—seemed a little too formal for class this morning.

"Haven't you saved up enough for a car?"

"A car, maybe. Insurance and gas? Not a chance. I'm tapped out as it is and the last thing I need is another thing in my life." Once she was satisfied with her outfit, she let out a heavy breath and looked around. "Okay, what are we doing?"

Leslie indicated a basket full of boxes of heart-shaped chocolates. The rejects from Valentine's Day. "Ronnie wants us to mark those down to half price. They each need to be stickered."

Kathy nodded and reached for the sticker gun. Grabbing a box of chocolates from the basket, she checked the price and then adjusted it on the gun. "I swear, Leslie, I'm going to lose my mind. How do people go to school full time for *four years*? And to work on top of it?" She shook her head. "I'll tell you one thing, I have a lot more respect for people like that. My sister worked her butt off to pay her way through. I couldn't do it."

"You kind of are, though," Leslie said. "And if you need a breather, I'd be happy to take a couple of your shifts. You know I could use the money."

"I know, but so could I."

"Not at the expense of your sanity."

Kathy smiled. "I guess that's true."

"Special delivery!" Ronnie called from across the store. She weaved her way through the racks of clothes holding a large bouquet of lilies. She set them on the register in front of Kathy. "Who's the admirer?"

"For me?" Kathy's eyes grew wide as she looked at the bouquet. They were beautiful. She had never gotten flowers like this before. And she didn't count the one dollar carnations they sold during lunch periods in high school.

"They were just dropped off by a courier," she said. "There's a card."

"I see you've scoped this out already," Leslie said with a laugh.

"You know it!"

Kathy reached for the card. It was from Jeremy, which made sense, but was still a surprise. He was never usually the romantic type. Then again, maybe he was making up for Valentine's Day. They had just officially gotten back together a week ago to the day.

Kathy,

I tried to find something as beautiful as you, but nothing comes close. Enjoy the lilies. I'm proud of everything you're doing.

- Jeremy

If she wasn't standing in the middle of the store with an audience of Leslie and Ronnie, she probably would've cried. Those simple words meant so much to her: *I'm proud of everything you're doing.* No matter how tired she had felt moments ago, she now felt like she could take on anything.

"That's sweet," Leslie said, reading over Kathy's shoulder.

She folded it quickly and slipped it back in the envelope.

"What does it say?" Ronnie asked.

"The usual sweetness," Leslie told her. "So are things going better the second time around?"

Kathy was still smiling at the flowers and it took her a moment to realize Leslie was asking her something.

"Huh? Oh, yeah, they are. It's still new. We've only been back together officially for a little while, but we're both different people now. It seems to be working."

"I'm glad," Leslie said.

Ronnie examined the flowers again. "A man who sends you treats at work sounds like a damn fine man to me. Hold on to him, honey."

Kathy laughed. "Would you mind putting these in the break room so they don't get ruined up here? I have to figure out how to get them home safely on the bus."

"I'll give you a ride home," Leslie said. "Don't worry about it."

"Thanks."

Kathy spent the next half hour labelling the discounted chocolates, then stacked them back in the basket and carried them to the display by the concourse door. Ronnie wanted them somewhere where people could see them and draw them in to the store for the deals.

As Kathy approached the opening to the concourse, she saw Steven sitting at a small table near the coffee kiosk in the middle of the concourse. She waved, but he didn't see her. A moment later, a blonde took the seat across from him and they both started talking. They exchanged smiles and both seemed relaxed. Familiar with each other.

Kathy busied herself with stacking the chocolates, keeping an eye on her brother-in-law and his mysterious friend. She didn't know who this woman was and she wondered if Samantha did. By time she finished with the display, Steven and the blonde had finished their coffee. Together, they walked down the concourse to the door, still awfully chummy with each other.

Kathy didn't like it one bit.

More by the Author

To find more books by the author, visit
DavidNethBooks.com/Books

* * *

Subscribe to his newsletter to be the first to know of new
releases and special deals!
DavidNethBooks.com/Newsletter

* * *

**If you enjoyed the book, please consider leaving a
review on Goodreads or the retailer you bought it from.**
Reviews help potential readers determine whether
they'll enjoy a book, so any comments on what you
thought of the story would be very helpful!

About the Author

David Neth is the author of the Coven series, the Under the Moon series, Heat series, the Fuse series, and other stories. He lives in Batavia, NY, where he dreams of a successful publishing career and opening his own bookstore.

Also writes small town romance as D. Allen.

www.DavidNethBooks.com

www.facebook.com/DavidNethBooks